Charlie Joe Jackson's Guide to Reading

HEY! Wait a sec— that's not right!

Tommy Greenwald

Charlie Joe Jackson's Guide to NOT Reading

Now that's more like it!

SQUARE FISH

Roaring Brook Press ✱ New York

For Cathy,

who gladly read several drafts of this book
and helped make it better.

And for Charlie, Joe, and Jack,

who didn't.

**SQUARE
FISH**

An Imprint of Macmillan

CHARLIE JOE JACKSON'S GUIDE TO NOT READING.
Text copyright © 2011 by Tommy Greenwald.
Illustrations copyright © 2011 by Roaring Brook Press.
All rights reserved. Printed in the United States of America by R. R. Donnelley & Sons Company,
Harrisonburg, Virginia. For information, address Square Fish, 175 Fifth Avenue, New York, NY 10010.

Square Fish and the Square Fish logo are trademarks of Macmillan and are used by
Roaring Brook Press under license from Macmillan.

Library of Congress Cataloging-in-Publication Data
Greenwald, Tom.
Charlie Joe Jackson's guide to not reading / Tom Greenwald.
p.   cm.
Summary: Middle schooler Charlie Joe is proud of his success at avoiding reading,
but eventually his schemes go too far.
ISBN 978-1-250-00337-9
[1. Books and reading—Fiction. 2. Middle schools—Fiction. 3. Schools—Fiction.
4. Interpersonal relations—Fiction. 5. Humorous stories.]   I. Title.
PZ7.G8523Ch 2011   [Fic]—dc22   2010024079

Originally published in the United States by Roaring Brook Press
First Square Fish Edition: May 2012
Square Fish logo designed by Filomena Tuosto
Book designed by Andrew Arnold
mackids.com
2 4 6 8 10 9 7 5 3
AR: 5.4 / LEXILE: 830L

Part One
HOW TO NOT READ

the plan:

AVOID
READING
at all cost!

My name is Charlie Joe Jackson, and I hate reading. And if you're reading this book, you hate reading, too.

In fact, you do whatever you can to avoid reading, and the fact that you're holding a book in your hand right now is kind of shocking.

I know exactly how you feel; I'm one of you.

Just remember: you are not alone. We'll get through this together.

This book is a guide for people like us.

It will serve two purposes.

One, it will show people how to get out of reading.

And two, on those unfortunate occasions when you're not able to get out of reading and are forced to read a book, it will be a nice easy book to read.

In all likelihood, you're reading this book against your will, and I sympathize with you. Therefore, I also make you this solemn promise:

The chapters will be short. The pages will be shorter. And whenever possible, I will keep the words shortest.

One syllable. Or less.

* * *

I'm also going to include some specific tips about reading—or NOT reading—throughout this book.

Some have to do with getting out of reading altogether, which is the strategy *I* recommend, and some have to do with making the best of it, if you do have to read a book. It can be surprisingly hard to avoid reading a book at some point in your life—even in middle school, as it turns out. You'll understand more as "our story unfolds." (One of my book-reading friends, Jake Katz, used that term once when he was describing a paper he was writing. He became somewhat less of a friend right at that moment.)

Charlie Joe's Tip #1

IF YOU HAVE TO READ A BOOK, MAKE SURE IT HAS SHORT CHAPTERS.

This first tip is pretty self-explanatory. Think about it. If your mom or dad tells you to read three chapters before bed, wouldn't you rather the chapters be one page each instead of ten pages each? Wouldn't you rather read three pages instead of thirty pages? That way, you're reading twenty-seven less pages, but you can still say, "Hey, guess what? I read my three chapters."

Trust me, they'll never know the difference.

I've hated reading for as far back as I can remember.

I didn't mind it when my mom read to me when I was little. That was fine because I could stay up later, and sometimes she even fell asleep in my bed, which I have to admit I actually liked at the time.

But then as I got a little older she started to say, "Okay, now you read the rest of the chapter," and that was just *so* not going to happen.

So I'd cry, and she'd read some more.

(By the way, I learned to cry on purpose that way. It's a useful skill. I've noticed that girls really like it when a guy gets teary sometimes—like at a movie where the hero makes a supreme sacrifice for his one true love, for example, because that means he's sensitive or something, and girls seem to like that. Personally, I prefer action movies where somebody blows something up, or a comedy where some chubby guy falls in love with a gorgeous lifeguard who only speaks French. That's more my speed.)

Anyway, the whole crying-in-front-of-Mom-so-I-wouldn't-have-to-read-it-myself thing, that worked great until I was about ten.

So here I am in middle school, and
I'm proud to say I *still* hate reading.

Which is how the whole mess began.

It started when I was supposed to read this book *Billy's
Bargain* for my English class. It's about this kid, Billy, and
the bargain he strikes with the Devil to pitch a no-hitter in
the championship game. But, it turns out the Devil is actually just a guy that was hired by Billy's dad to pretend to be
the Devil, because Billy's dad figures that if Billy thinks he
made a deal with the Devil to pitch a no-hitter, then Billy
would have the confidence to actually pitch a no-hitter.

It's not as complicated as I just made it sound. It's apparently a pretty good book, according to my teacher, Ms.
Ferrell. And I guess it's got one of those just-believe-in-
yourself-and-others-will-believe-in-you-too messages that
grown-ups want kids to hear over and over.

Anyway, like I said, that's where I ran into trouble.

✳✳✳

I did what I usually do. I read the back cover, the
front inside flap, the first chapter, and the last chapter.

Then I sat next to my friend Timmy McGibney at lunch.

For about two years, Timmy and I had what you might call an "arrangement." I would buy him an ice-cream sandwich, and he would tell me all about what was in the rest of the book. It was a "win-win" situation, which is one of those weird expressions my parents use all the time.

Naturally, I figured we'd make the same deal we always made.

"So Timmy," I said, handing him his ice-cream sandwich, "*Billy's Bargain* was a pretty good book."

"How would you know?" he asked. He always asked me that. It was kind of a routine we had.

"Well, the beginning and the ending were pretty good."

"I guess so," Timmy said. He was fiddling with his lacrosse stick. Lacrosse was the only thing he loved more than ice-cream sandwiches.

"Tryouts coming up, huh," I said, pointing at his stick.

"Yup," he said. I waited for him to say something else, but he didn't. This was weird. Usually he could talk about lacrosse for hours.

Timmy wolfed down his ice-cream sandwich and looked at mine. "I'm actually really hungry today," he said. "Really, really hungry."

I suddenly got a pretty uneasy feeling. "What do you mean, 'really, really hungry'?"

"I'm saying I'm so hungry I could eat two ice-cream sandwiches," Timmy said. "Maybe three."

I looked at him in disbelief. We'd had the same deal going for almost a year. I'd handed over enough free ice cream for him to start his own dairy farm. Now all of a sudden he was pulling this!

I looked around. I checked my pocket for money. I considered my options. Then I did the only thing I could do.

I bought him another ice-cream sandwich.

* * *

After lunch I went to the library and looked up the word *blackmail* just to make sure I understood exactly what was happening.

The librarian, Ms. Reedy, was an old friend of mine, even though she represented everything evil. Back in the old days, she was the librarian at my elementary school, and she used to try anything to get me to read. One time in first grade, she sat me down and had me listen to a song called "Grab a Book and Go," all about the joys of reading. One of the verses went "Snuggle in your bed, the day is near its end. All alone, but you're not alone, a book can be a friend."

I've never quite forgiven her.

So needless to say, she gave me quite the double take when I walked in.

"Charlie Joe," she said, "did you take a wrong turn somewhere?"

I laughed. (Always good to laugh at an adult's jokes, regardless of whether they're funny or not.)

"I just need to look something up," I answered, trying to keep the conversation to a minimum so I could take care of business and get out of there.

Ms. Reedy looked at me and winked.

"Well don't worry, Charlie Joe, your secret is safe with me," she said.

I just looked at the previous

chapter and realized it was way too long. I just ignored
Charlie Joe's Tip #1!

Sorry about that. Won't happen again.

Charlie Joe's Tip #2

NEVER READ A BOOK BY SOMEONE WHOSE NAME YOU CAN'T PRONOUNCE.

Let's face it: chances are you wouldn't be reading this book if it were called *Venedkyt Styokierwski's Guide to Not Reading.*

And I sure wouldn't be writing it.

My point is, if you have to read, it's really important to make sure the cover doesn't scare you in any way. And that starts with the author's name. It has to be reader friendly.

Like Charlie Joe Jackson, for example.

VS.

When I got home from school that day, I was still annoyed about Timmy's power move. Two ice-cream sandwiches! What's next, a Carvel Fudgie the Whale cake?

I threw down my ridiculously heavy backpack—there should be a law against ridiculously heavy backpacks, by the way—and made myself a bowl of cereal.

Then I considered my options:

> 1. *doing homework, which involved reading; or*
> 2. *playing with the dogs.*

Not a hard choice.

We have two dogs: Moose and Coco. They're both lab mixes. We rescued them from the pound.

They have a great life: eat, sleep, play, and absolutely no reading of any kind.

I'm sure it won't surprise you to learn that occasionally I get jealous of both of them.

After I threw them the tennis ball approximately 4,386 times, I managed to forget all about Timmy McGibney and his ice-cream sandwiches.

Temporarily.

Charlie Joe's Tip #3

THERE ARE ALWAYS WAYS TO GET OUT OF READING.

Here's a short list:

1. *Sleep.*
2. *Clean your room.*
3. *Pretend to clean your room.*
4. *Go outside. Parents love it when you go outside.*
5. *Practice an instrument. Even if you don't play one. Parents love it when you practice music without having to be nagged about it.*
6. *Eat. (My personal favorite.)*
7. *Feed your book to the dog.*
8. *Clean up the dog's throw-up.*
9. *Run away from home. (Only in extreme cases.)*
10. *Plead insanity.*

"So are you going to tell me what was in the middle of the book, or aren't you?"

It was the next day, and I was following Timmy and his lacrosse stick around the cafeteria. He still wasn't telling me what happened in the middle of *Billy's Bargain*, and I was starting to panic. I'd bought him two ice-cream sandwiches, a slice of pizza, and three chocolate milks, but nothing.

I suddenly realized that this wasn't about free food. Something else was bothering Timmy, and I needed to find out what it was.

My non-reading future depended on it.

The first thing to do was to find Katie Friedman, who'd been my best friend from kindergarten to fourth grade, which was when I suddenly realized you weren't allowed to have a girl best friend.

But even though we technically weren't best friends anymore, I still told her everything, and in times of crisis she was still my go-to problem solver. I've found that in matters of feelings and thinking, girls seem to have a handle on things that guys just don't. They seem to care more. Or maybe they're just less afraid to admit it.

And Katie Friedman cares more than everyone else. She gets what you're telling her, and probably understands what you're talking about more than you do.

I guess you could say she "reads between the lines," which is an expression that's meant as a compliment, even though it has the word *reads* in it.

But I don't mean to suggest that I'm in love with her or anything. I'm not. Like I said, we're just best friends—or would be, if that sort of thing were allowed.

At any rate, I found her in her usual spot, back left corner of the cafeteria by the vending machines, texting the girls right next to her. (You aren't allowed to text in school, but at recess and lunch everybody snuck in a few.)

I quietly called her over. She put away her phone and followed me around the corner.

"What's up?"

Katie was the only one who knew about the deal that Timmy and I had. (She was a big reader and constantly told me what a loser I was for hating books, but she gave

me points for creativity.) I quickly filled her in on what was going on, and how for some reason all the ice-cream sandwiches in the world weren't going to make Timmy tell me what was in the middle of that freakin' book.

She looked at me. Then she laughed.

I was shocked. "What? WHAT?!?!"

She shook her head. "You are so clueless. Why are boys so clueless? Why do they never notice the real things that are going on in the world? It's bad enough that you refuse to read, Charlie Joe. But would it kill you to go to a movie every once in a while where something actually meaningful happens, instead of some chubby guy falling in love with a gorgeous lifeguard who only speaks French?" (She knew me pretty well.) "You might actually learn something about psychology." (Katie had recently decided she wanted to be a therapist when she got older, like her parents.)

I wanted so badly to come up with something smart and psychologically impressive to say in return.

But all I could come up with was, "Chubby guys falling for gorgeous lifeguards who only speak French are funny."

Katie smiled. One of the things I loved about her was that whenever she yelled at me, she always felt really guilty right afterward. And this time, she felt guilty enough to give me the piece of information I'd come looking for.

"The problem isn't Timmy. It's Eliza."

Charlie Joe's Tip #4

IF YOU WANT GIRLS TO LIKE YOU, DON'T READ.

Girls think it's kind of cool if you don't read a lot and still get good grades.

It's kind of like, you're smart but you don't even try.

As opposed to the kids who work really hard and get good grades, or the kids who don't work at all and get bad grades. Girls don't really like either of those kinds of boys.

So if you want to get girls, it's important to read as little as possible and still do well in school.

Here's how:

1. *Participate in class. Ask a lot of questions. Seem really enthusiastic.*
2. *Turn in all your homework on time.*
3. *Make sure a friend of yours is assigned the same book. And make sure he's actually reading it.*
4. *Bring pictures of your dogs to school and show them to your teachers. Make sure the pictures show the dogs doing cute*

things—the kind of things that get on YouTube.

5. *Don't get in trouble at lunch.*
6. *Don't get in trouble at recess.*
7. *If the book you're supposed to read was turned into a movie, rent the movie.*
8. *If the book you're supposed to read was turned into an audio book, listen to the audio book. (It counts as reading, but it's not!)*
9. *Make sure you get great grades in the classes that don't involve reading—like gym.*
10. *Partner with someone really smart in science.*
11. *Read the first and last chapters of all assigned books.*
12. *(Extra Credit) Always do the extra credit, as long as it doesn't involve reading.*

"Eliza" is Eliza Collins.

Although to be technical about it, she's one of those girls who doesn't really need a last name. Like Beyoncé.

That's because Eliza has been crowned "the prettiest girl in the grade."

She took over the title in about fourth grade and has held it ever since. You know the type: looks like a magazine model, popular, and there always seems to be like a swirl of energy and hair-brushing and giggling everywhere she stands. People can just be walking by and they get sucked in like she's the center of a tornado or something. (I actually made up a song for her a couple of years ago when I first saw her in action. "Hurricane Eliza comin' in, the hottest hurricane in town, you'll get blown away when Hurricane Eliza's comin' down." The tune I came up with is pretty catchy, but you can't hear it, because this is a book— another problem with books by the way.)

Rumor has it she's already been offered a job modeling in Spain next year.

(Not just "modeling," mind you, but "modeling in Spain." As if just "modeling" isn't enough.) She walks around in school like she owns the place, which, in a way, she does. And she tends to want the things she can't have—a pet cheetah, a driver's license . . . me.

That's right, you heard correctly.

ME!

But here's what's weird. Even though she's totally hot (and she really is, that long blond hair is no joke), and even though she thinks I'm totally adorable (I didn't say it, she did) . . . unlike the rest of Western civilization, *I don't have a crush on her.*

I don't know why, I just don't.

You know how when you can have something so easily, you don't necessarily want it? Like when you can only have one bowl of ice cream after dinner, you desperately want more, but if your mom says you can have the whole carton, suddenly you're like, I'm kind of sick of ice cream? Well, it was like that with Eliza.

She was the whole carton. All the time.

* * *

So when Katie said *Eliza*, I was confused. I wasn't sure what any of this had to do with Timmy. As far as I could tell he hadn't really discovered girls yet . . . and perhaps more to the point, they hadn't really discovered him.

I looked at Katie. "I don't get it. Timmy doesn't like Eliza."

Katie was still laughing at me. "For a pretty smart guy, Charlie Joe, you can be pretty thick sometimes."

Was that a compliment or an insult?

"It's not Eliza that Timmy's worried about. It's her dad."

I thought for a second. "Mr. Collins?" I said, brilliantly.

"Yup," Katie said. "He's the boys' lacrosse coach, right?"

Katie played lacrosse. She was pretty good, too. (I could add "for a girl" here, but I won't.)

I shrugged. "I think so. Why?"

She leaned in, as if to say, *Here comes the good part.*

"Apparently Timmy thinks that because Eliza likes you, she'll tell her dad to pick you for the team, and you might make it instead of him. He's totally freaked out about it."

I couldn't believe it. It was hard to make the travel lacrosse team, but Timmy had been practicing for weeks. Meanwhile, I'd barely ever picked up a stick before. I was just going out for the team to hang out with my friends.

"That's ridiculous," I said.

"It's true," Katie said back.

"I'll talk to Eliza about it," I suggested.

"NO!" Katie answered immediately. "That would be the worst thing you could do. Timmy doesn't want anyone

23

to know how insecure he is. Just keep your mouth shut about it."

I still wasn't convinced. "Where did you hear this?" I demanded.

"Don't worry about it. Let it go."

By now Katie's friends were calling to her to come back, and she started walking back toward them, already texting them. Then she turned back to me with a mischievous look in her eyes.

"Hey, I have a crazy idea that could solve your whole problem!"

"What's that?" I said, hopefully.

Katie smacked me on the shoulder. "Read the book."

✳ ✳ ✳

I thought about what Katie said and weighed my options.

I could just let the whole thing go, read *Billy's Bargain* and be done with it.

Or I could ignore Katie's advice, talk to Eliza, try to get her to talk to her dad, make sure Timmy made the team, and not have to read *Billy's Bargain*.

Not a difficult decision.

Charlie Joe's Tip #5

IF ANYONE—LIKE, SAY, A PARENT—EVER YELLS AT YOU FOR NOT READING, JUST POINT OUT TO THEM ALL THE MANY WAYS YOU DO READ.

1. *Web sites*
2. *Instant messages*
3. *Texts*
4. *Video game instructions*
5. *Sports scores*
6. *Menus*
7. *The viewer's guide on the TV*
8. *The back of the cereal box*
9. *T-shirts*
10. *Supermarket coupons*
11. *Road signs*

So you know how I called Eliza Collins hot? Well, my parents hate it when I use the word *hot* to describe girls. They think it's insulting, "degrading" my mom says, "shallow" my dad says, like I think it's the only important thing. I get it, I get it, brains matter, too.

But let me let you in on a little secret: girls LOVE it when you call them hot.

Especially really smart girls. Really smart, brainiac girls love it more than any other kind of girl when you call them hot.

But, out of respect to my mom and all the other girls out there who don't like the term *hot*, I will not use the word anymore from here on in.

Eliza Collins (non-brainiac) has been called hot—I mean gorgeous—her whole life, so she really knows it, and she acts like it. If our school was the universe, and the girls in our school were the solar system, then she'd be the sun. And the moon. She's always surrounded by girls, by boys, even by some teachers who, although they would never admit it, like to be liked by the popular kids.

If you wanted to see Eliza, you had to make an appointment.

I was slightly different I guess, because for some reason—like I said—she liked me. BUT . . . she also hated me, because she liked me, and I didn't like her. Her inability to snag me was her one imperfection, her one blemish, like the annoying cherry on top of an otherwise perfect hot fudge sundae.

So of course, she made me suffer.

✳ ✳ ✳

The next day at lunch, I told Talia, one of Eliza's "assistants," that I needed to talk to Eliza. She looked at me like I had two heads.

"I'm pretty sure Eliza doesn't want to talk to you," Talia said, barely looking up from her low-fat turkey burger and high-fat large fries. (Girls are complicated.)

extra LOW fat

extra LARGE

This was important. No time for pride. I placed my hand on her shoulder. "Tell her it's important."

See, the thing about Talia—and a lot of girls, I've noticed—is that they love it when you touch them. I know that sounds gross, but I don't mean it in that way. I just mean, show them some gentle affection, show them that you care about them and you're "there" for them (whatever that means), and suddenly they're your best friend.

In particular, I've noticed that girls really love the gentle hand on the shoulder.

It's brotherly, but manly.

Does that make them shallow, like all they're looking for is affection? I don't think so. I just think it makes them seem more human.

It's one of the good, human things about girls.

✳ ✳ ✳

Talia felt my hand on her shoulder, then looked up at me. I could literally feel her shoulders relax as she smiled at me. Then she opened up a little pink book.

"I think she has an opening tomorrow after math," she said.

Meanwhile, the due date for the assignment was coming up fast, and I was still without an outline from Timmy. I could've read the book, sure, but then my perfect record would've been broken. I'm not gonna lie; I'm proud of my perfect record. All the kids knew about it, and were mighty impressed.

And let me tell you another thing—I'm no quitter. I was *committed* to not reading and it was going to take more than just some dumb lacrosse team misunderstanding for me to throw in the towel.

See, it wasn't just that I was lazy.

It was that I didn't want to disappoint my fans.

Charlie Joe's Tip #6

READING WON'T HELP YOU SUCCEED IN LIFE.

My parents say that if I don't start reading, I'll do badly on all the reading and writing tests that help you get into a good college. And if I don't get into a good college, I'll probably end up a failure in life. At least twice a week they say to me, "How are you going to get into a good college if you don't read? And if you don't get into a good college, you'll end up _____."
(Anything from "homeless" to "a criminal"—it varies with their moods).

My first answer to that is, RELAX. I'm only in middle school, people.

My second answer is, what if I'm amazing at some weird thing that nobody else is interested in? Won't that help me get into a good college?

I briefly considered signing up for mime class, kind of as a goof. But it turned out that there's no one less goofy than a mime-boy, do they take it seriously. You would think they would realize how ridiculous it is, but no. It's too bad that it was such a drag and so embarrassing, because it didn't seem particularly hard. And my guess is that there are very few kids who put "master mime" on their college applications.

Maybe I should take up fencing. It's like sword fighting, only you don't get killed. Fencing has clothes that are really cool, it's all about handling a weapon for crying out loud, what could be better than that, and it's just weird enough to look great on those all-important college applications. What's the down side?

Touché!

During math class, the only thing I could think about was my appointment with Eliza, and getting her to make sure that Timmy made the travel lacrosse team so that he would be my friend again. Then as soon as that drama was out of the way, he'd give me the run-down on what was in the middle of *Billy's Bargain*, I could write my paper without reading it, and order would be restored to the universe.

I know it's hard to believe, but all this excitement made it very difficult for me to concentrate on the fractional ratios of binary numbers.

(Don't bother looking up "fractional ratios of binary numbers," by the way. I just made it up.)

* * *

Finally, class was over. I went out into the hall, where Eliza was being attended to by a harem of three Elizettes.

She saw me and shooed away her friends.

"Why, Charlie Joe Jackson, as I live and breathe." She

proceeded to breathily give me a kiss on the cheek to really drive home the "live and breathe" part.

She was kind of dramatic that way.

"Hey, Lize," I said. (Pronounced *lies*. Only those in the inner circle got to call her that.)

She swung her hair over to one side. Whenever she did that, activity in the hallway pretty much ground to a halt. It was kind of amazing, I had to admit—like when you see a red Maserati on the street and everyone stops to stare.

"Now, Charlie, are you here to ask me to the end of the year dance?"

The end of the year dance was like four months away, and for anyone else, that would have been a ridiculous question. But this was Eliza Collins. For all I know, several kids had asked her already.

"Isn't it a little early to be thinking about the end of the year dance?" I asked.

Eliza brushed a single golden strand of hair out of her left eye. "Well, I was just making sure. Because if you're about to ask me out or something, you know you're barking up the wrong hill."

She had this way of mangling expressions that for some reason actually made her hotter.

"I figured that, Lize. I'm actually here on behalf of someone else."

Her eyes narrowed. Not a good sign. I plunged ahead, whispering so the entire hall couldn't hear me.

"You know Timmy McGibney, right?" (Duh. Of course she knew Timmy McGibney.) "Anyway, I happen to know for a fact that he is a really good lacrosse player, and if you maybe talked to your dad about making sure he made the travel team, that would be such a totally huge favor to me, because I know how much it means to Timmy. And I promise I'll never ask you for another favor again as long as I live."

✳ ✳ ✳

Have you ever noticed that really pretty girls think being pretty is like a license to talk loud? Especially when they get irritated?

Eliza was irritated, because not only was I not asking her out, I was asking her for a favor that she found really . . . well, boring.

Eliza heard my plea, and then said loud enough for people in Thailand to hear, "CHARLIE JOE. THAT IS SO SWEET THAT YOU CARE ABOUT YOUR FRIEND TIMMY THAT MUCH. BUT I DON'T KNOW ANYTHING ABOUT MY DAD'S LACROSSE TEAM, AND TO TELL YOU THE TRUTH, I REALLY DON'T CARE. SO, YEAH, UH . . . NO." And she swung her hair back to the other side, then walked away.

Everyone in the hallway stared as she left me standing there, mission completely unaccomplished.

* * *

So, to recap: a) Eliza said no; b) Timmy probably would never read another book for me again; and c) the entire hallway pretty much thought that I thought that Timmy wasn't good enough to make the lacrosse team on his own.

Oops.

Charlie Joe's Tip #7

READING CAN RUIN FRIENDSHIPS.

The thing I've noticed about reading is that it can become a habit. A bad habit, like smoking, or forgetting to put on deodorant, or saying "you know" all the time. (Or "Yeah, no" to start a sentence. I hate that one. What does that even mean?)

Take my buddy Jake Katz, who used to take pride in not reading, just like me.

Then he got this book about snakes, fell in love, and started reading books about reptiles all the time.

Then he started reading about all kinds of things—weather patterns, Civil War battles, science fiction stories, murder mysteries, even a book called *Mastering the Art of Slicing Sushi*.

Like he's ever going to need to know that.

Now, Jake carries books around with him everywhere, no matter where he's going. The minute things are quiet, or he has time to kill between activities, he whips one out and starts reading right there and then.

I'm not gonna lie, it's put a strain on our friendship.

Later at recess, while I was trying to get over my failure with Eliza, I was cornered by my English teacher, Ms. Ferrell.

"Hi there, Charlie Joe."

"Hi, Ms. Ferrell." I tapped my foot impatiently. Recess was 24 minutes long, and every minute was like gold.

"Charlie Joe, have you read *Billy's Bargain* yet? You know the paper is due next week. I expect big things from you on this paper."

It was my curse to be one of those students that Ms. Ferrell thought showed promise. I hate *promise*. It's just a synonym for *high expectations*, which are almost impossible to meet.

What's so great about "great"?

"Pretty good" is good enough for me.

I looked longingly at my buddies, who were playing a rare form of basketball that involved whipping the ball at each other's groinal regions. I saw Phil Manning nail Ricky Snyder, and I couldn't help but crack up.

"Charlie Joe, I asked you a question." Ms. Ferrell leaned in close enough that I could tell she'd had the fish sticks for lunch. (At least we had *that* in common.)

"I'm pretty much halfway through it." Halfway through the first chapter, that is.

She sighed that classic teacher sigh.

"Fine. I look forward to reading your observations. And no more excuses. If your paper's late, it's ten points off. Rules are rules."

I may have forgotten to mention that in addition to being allergic to reading, I also had an occasional problem with punctuality when it came to assignments.

Ms. Ferrell adjusted her glasses, which was a sure sign that she was coming to the heart of the matter.

"Charlie Joe, someone of your ability has the responsibility to produce a paper worthy of your talents, however hidden they may be. I've talked about this with your mom and dad several times. They're wonderful people, and you really owe it to them to start applying yourself before it's too late."

Wow. She played the parents card. That was low.

And with that she walked off to join her fellow teachers, who were technically assigned to watch kids at recess but who really spent the time flirting with each other.

I made it over to my friends just in time for Pete Milano to throw a Spalding indoor-outdoor adult-sized basketball, and nail me right in my you-know-what.

The day was not turning out well.

Charlie Joe's Tip #8

NOT ALL BOOKS ARE BAD.

Every once in a while, a book can be a good thing. Here are those rare exceptions:

1. *Comic books*
2. *Yearbooks*
3. *Checkbooks (when your grandparents are writing you a check for your birthday)*
4. *Facebook (when your parents aren't looking)*

Since you're about to meet my

family, I may as well tell you a little bit about them.

The first thing I'll say is that they're pretty awesome.

My dad, James Jackson. Jimmy Jackson to his friends, although I once heard someone actually call him J.J. (It's as bad as when some lame adult who doesn't know me calls me C.J.) He's a lawyer, works a lot, likes to walk around the house in his boxers, has the eating habits of a ten-year-old, and makes really strange noises when he plays with the dogs. He loves ketchup but hates tomatoes. He's not tall or short or big or small—he's a pretty regular, normal-looking dad. I guess I kind of look like him.

my Parents

My mom, Claire Jackson. Homemaker/substitute teacher, works a lot, orders me and my sister to stay in touch with her but then never answers her cell phone, laughs at all of dad's jokes even when they're not funny, does a killer Australian accent, rolls her eyes when dad makes funny noises when he plays with the dogs, tells him to put clothes on, and eats the to-matoes off his plate. She's super nice, and all my friends say she's really pretty. When they say that, it kind of grosses me out and makes me feel proud at the same time.

My sister, Megan Jackson. Two years older than me, used to be a tomboy until she discovered boys, wears shorts shorter than my underwear, plays a mean clarinet, LOVES TO READ.

So yeah, even though in most books this would proba-bly be the part where the narrator complains about his family, talks about how miserable life is at home, and pleads for the reader's sympathy, it turns out I really like my fam-ily. They're pretty cool. I like every one of them pretty much all the time. Even my sister. I know it's crazy, but it's true.

In other words, no big family drama situation.

At least, not until I got home that night.

My sister, Megan

The afternoon started innocently enough. After school I went over to my friend Jake's house, where I found him standing in his yard, reading a book.

It's hard enough to read a book, but reading *standing up*?

Fortunately, the one thing that can get Jake's nose out of a book is Xbox—it's *just that good*—so we headed inside to play.

But his mom met us at the door, announced it was a beautiful day, and told us to go back outside.

So we stayed outside for three minutes, then went around to the other side of the house, snuck in through the side door, went downstairs to the basement, and played Xbox.

In the middle of the game I got this weird text from Timmy: Read any good books lately?

I texted back: Haha what do you think? and forgot all about it.

After about forty-five awesome Xbox minutes, Jake's dog gave us away by barking furiously at one of the Nazi Zombies. His mom chased us outside again.

So we went outside and hung out in his front yard for about an hour, talking about Nazi Zombies.

Then Jake said, "So, how come you don't like Eliza?"

Jake was incredibly smart, but he wasn't exactly Einstein with the girls, so he couldn't understand why anyone wouldn't like a girl who already liked him.

Especially a girl who looked like Eliza.

"It's hard to explain," I answered. "I wish I did like her though. It would make life so much easier."

"I don't think life is supposed to be easy," said the kid who's never gotten less than an A in his entire life.

Little did I know.

* * *

I knew something was wrong right when I got home, when I walked in the door and Moose and Coco didn't run up to greet me as if I was the only human being in the world that had ever existed.

The thing about dogs is, they pretty much reflect the mood in the house. If someone's sad, they're sad. If someone's happy, they're happy. And if someone's mad, which happened to be the case in this particular instance, they hide.

I made my way to the kitchen for my usual pre-dinner bowl of cereal. I like my stomach to be prepped with a solid snack before a sit-down meal.

I stopped in my tracks when I saw my mom sitting at the table with Timmy's mom.

Now, under normal circumstances, I love Ms. McGibney. She has, like, the best snack cabinet in the entire town: chips, chocolate-covered pretzels, cheese-covered popcorn, cookies galore, literally every kind of junk food that I want to eat and my mom will not buy. Plus, Ms. McGibney is always happy to drive Timmy and me anywhere.

But these were not normal circumstances. In fact they were highly abnormal.

Almost paranormal.

I gave a quick wave as I tried to sneak by them on my way to the cereal container.

"Hi, Ms. McGibney."

She smiled semi-brightly. "Hello, Charlie Joe dear."

My mom interrupted the pleasantries. "Charlie Joe, the

Captain Crunch/Fruit Loops combo platter will have to wait. Please come over here and sit down."

I sat. Coco went into the other room—she hated confrontation. Moose stuck around, looking at me like, "I really feel badly for you, but at the same time, I'm so glad I'm not you right now."

My mom folded her hands in that universal mom sign for *I'm talking and you're listening.*

"Rose has come here today with some very disturbing news."

* * *

Do you want me to go on, or should I end the chapter here? Are you desperate to know what happens, or are you more desperate to finish the chapter, put the book away and go watch TV?

I'd say we should take a vote, but since that's kind of impossible, I'll just put myself in your shoes. What would I want? How would I vote?

That settles it. End of chapter.

Charlie Joe's Tip #9

READING CAN MAKE YOU FAT.

Surely you've heard all about the studies that show how kids today just sit around eating candy and cheeseburgers, and how obesity among young people is a huge national problem. I think one of the cable news channels called it "An American epidemic of fatness," which sounds almost as scary as global warming.

Well, do you know what a major contributor to all that fat is?

Reading.

I'll have you know that reading burns absolutely no calories whatsoever.

So the next time you consider picking up a book, you might want to remember what an unhealthy choice you're making.

It's for your own good.

As my mother stared at me across the kitchen table, it suddenly occurred to me what happened.

When something interesting happens at school, kids like to talk about it.

Who knew?

It turns out that after Eliza and I had our little chat, Eliza immediately told her friend Talia about it. And Talia told this kid Adam about it. Then Adam told Becky, Becky told David, David told Emily, Emily told Eric, and Eric told Cathy . . . who happens to be Timmy's sister.

And Cathy told her mother. Who happens to be Timmy's mother.

And Timmy's mother told my mother.

And my mother told me, but good.

At first it sounded perfectly harmless. "So let me get this straight," she said, even though we were both pretty sure she had it straight. "You asked Eliza Collins to talk to her father about making sure Timmy made the lacrosse team?"

"Yup," I said. "What's the big deal? I was just trying to be a good friend."

My mom sighed heavily, which usually meant the beginning of the end.

"A good friend who wants someone to keep reading his books for him, apparently."

Uh-oh.

"Timmy told me all about your little arrangement, dear," Ms. McGibney said, almost apologetically.

I started to sweat. "What did he tell you?" I asked, needlessly.

Mom took this one. "In exchange for you buying Timmy food at lunch, he tells you what's in the book that you've been assigned to read. So you don't have to read it."

Then she waited for me to confirm or deny. What could I do?

"Oh," I confirmed.

But she wasn't done. "And according to Timmy, this has been going on for several years, and in all that time you pretty much haven't read even ONE of the books that you were supposed to read."

Wow. Timmy had really gone into the gory details. He must have been really upset that I talked to Eliza. Or, more accurately, he must have been really upset that the whole school found out that I talked to Eliza.

Dang it, I thought to myself, Katie was right. As usual.

"It's not that simple," I said. "I read parts of the books. I read all of the first chapters, and some of the second chapters, and most of the endings and stuff. I was really completely able to get the point of these books for sure. Timmy just helped me fill in some of the details, that's all."

Yeah, that wasn't gonna fly.

My mom looked at me with real disappointment, which made me feel terrible. "We'll talk more about this when Dad gets home."

Great. Something else to look forward to.

Mrs. McGibney took a sip of her cider, which reminded me that I had absolutely no saliva in my mouth and was dying of thirst. Her eyes were full of pity as she said the one thing she knew would make me feel at least a tiny bit better.

"I want you to know, Charlie Joe, that Timmy is going to be in just as much trouble as you are."

Charlie Joe's Tip #10

IT'S EASY TO CONVINCE OTHERS THAT YOU DO IN FACT READ, EVEN IF YOU DO IN FACT DON'T.

There are plenty of ways to come across as a book lover. Just follow these simple steps:

1. *Have a bookshelf in your room. Stock it with books.*
2. *Wear glasses—even if you don't need them.*
3. *Use the word* therefore *a lot.*
4. *Put a Harry Potter poster up on your wall.*
5. *Keep a library card handy at all times.*
6. *Ask for a gift certificate to Amazon for your birthday. (Don't worry, they sell DVDs.)*
7. *Get a shirt with a picture of Mark Twain on it.*
8. *Hang out at Barnes & Noble. (Great hot chocolate.)*
9. *Make your local library's Web site the homepage on your computer.*
10. *PERHAPS MOST IMPORTANT: Don't annoy or embarrass your friend who's reading all your books for you. **EVER.***

Can a book be divided into quarters, kind of like a football game? I think this is the end of the first quarter. Let's go to commercial break.

Part Two
THE LOVE OF MY LIFE AND OTHER IMPOSSIBILITIES

You know the expression "read it and weep"?

Whoever came up with that is a genius.

Charlie Joe's Tip #11

BOOKS THAT ARE DIVIDED INTO PARTS SHOULD BE AVOIDED AT ALL COSTS.

Except this one.

It's very difficult to sit there facing your mom and dad and be told you did something wrong, which in fact you did, and come up with some kind of quick, clever comeback.

So perhaps you'll forgive me for what I came up with, after listening to my mom tell my dad the whole story, and listening to my dad ask me what I had to say for myself:

"I am so, so sorry, and I swear, it will so totally never ever happen again."

I know, brilliant, right?

I'll spare you the details of my shameless pleas for mercy—it's possible a tear or two might even have leaked from my left eye—and cut right to the part where my dad announced the punishment. "Grounded—one week."

I could live with that, not so bad.

Then my mom chimed in. "Set the table, two weeks."

Well, now that seemed a little extreme.

"Load the dishwasher, three weeks," she continued.

Wait, what? This I could not let stand.

"Load the dishwasher for three weeks?!" I stammered. "That's crazy; that's so not fair! Not only do I get punished, Megan gets rewarded? How is that fair?"

My dad did that thing where his eyes suddenly get real narrow, and it occurred to me that I might have been a little out of line, jumping in to complain when the emotions were still raw. I waited nervously.

"Oh, you don't think it's fair, do you? Fine. We'll skip that one," he offered.

Wait . . . had my plea actually worked?

"Instead, we'll go with no cell phone for a month. And that actually works out really well since they don't allow cell phones at the public library anyway, which is where you'll be spending every day after school."

Um, can we go back to the whole dishwasher thing?

I know you feel my pain on this one, but
I have to say this anyway. It's impossible to overstate the
importance of the cell phone in a person's life.

Especially if that person is grounded and has a paper
due in five days.

Actually, technically in four and a half days.

Charlie Joe's Tip #12

THE LIBRARY CAN BE YOUR FRIEND.

Don't automatically assume that just because the library is filled with books it's a bad place.

It all depends on why you're going there.

For example, there's a pretty good movie section in most libraries. And they have computers.

The library in my town even has a place to buy snacks. I like to grab a book (that I have no intention of reading), then amble over to the café for a little hot chocolate and conversation.

Every once in a while I'll even open the book.

Sometimes, a girl I know will wander over and ask me what I'm reading. (Unless she goes to my school, in which case she'll know that books and I don't get along.) Then I'll ask her what she's reading. Then I'll ask her lots of questions about her book, which shows how curious and sensitive I am. Then I'll say it sounds like a book I might like. She'll smile. I'll smile back.

Yeah—like I said, the library can be your friend.

20

The library can also be your mortal enemy.

Take the girl out of the equation, add your mother and your sister, and a complete lack of texting, and the library becomes a kind of hell on earth. A pit of despair. A black hole of desperation and misery.

A place you don't want to be, especially on a *Saturday*.

But that Saturday—the day after my little kitchen table chat with Mom and Ms. McGibney—I was sitting in the Eastport Public Hell on Earth, with a copy of *Billy's Bargain* in my hand.

I tried to find a corner of the library where I wouldn't be seen, because I had a reputation to uphold.

And then—believe it or not—I started reading.

LIBRARY

PUBLIC LIBRARY
"Your mortal enemy!"

So, yeah, this should be the place in the book where I tell you that it turns out that the book was amazing, time flew by, and all of a sudden I looked up and it was eight o'clock. I had discovered the joys of reading and storytelling, and the characters spoke to me, and not only did I want to read more books, I wanted to move into the library.

Only, that's not what happened AT ALL.

Listen, I've got nothing against *Billy's Bargain*, or the guy who wrote it, some guy named Ted Hauser. I'm sure Ted Hauser is a perfectly nice man with a great family, and congratulations to him for writing a book that most kids seem to enjoy. I'm sure his mom is really proud of him and brags about him at dinner parties.

But, no matter how nice a guy and how successful an author Ted Hauser is, I'm pretty sure that doesn't give him the right to ruin my life.

After two hours—and believe me, I was counting, pretty much a second at a time—I realized I had read eighteen pages.

Now, I'm no expert—in fact, far from it—but I'm pretty

sure eighteen pages in two hours is not record-setting speed.

At this rate, I was going to finish the book in about three years.

I felt a tap on my shoulder. It was my sister, Megan, who had four—count 'em, FOUR!—books in her hands.

"How's it going? Are you getting anywhere? Are you enjoying the book?"

Sometimes, having a nice sister is no better than having a mean sister. Trust me, sometimes it's worse.

I looked up at her and rubbed my eyes. "Oh yeah, I'm cruising along. It's actually really good."

"I'll bet it is."

I looked around at everyone else in the library, seemingly there of their own free will. Who were these people who seemed to actually enjoy the act of just sitting there, doing nothing but looking at words on a page, and somehow finding some sense of happiness or joy or satisfaction or fulfillment? There were even people reading the newspaper, for crying out loud. The newspaper! When you could go online and catch three quick headlines that tell you everything you might need to know. (War, peace, disaster, a new 3-D movie premiere—it's all just a click away, thanks to the good people at Google.)

Who were these people, and what was I doing here with them?

Megan sat down next to me. "Listen. I'll make you a deal. This is probably the stupidest thing I'll ever do in my life, and I'm sure I'll regret it forever—"

She stopped—a second-thoughts kind of stop.

Go on. Go ON!!! My mouth didn't say it, but my brain was screaming it.

"I can't stand seeing you this mopey. I know you're in a time crunch. I'll read the book for you tonight. This one time, and that's it. From now on, you read your own books. READ THE BOOKS!"

Like I said. Sometimes having a nice sister is the best freakin' thing in the world.

A BRIEF TRIBUTE TO MY AWESOME SISTER

The funny thing about Megan Jackson is that she is completely not funny. She has zero sense of humor, she can't tell a joke to save her life, and she doesn't get what's funny about *The Simpsons*, which is just sad.

Let's call her comically challenged.

But—and I've racked my brain about this, believe me—that's the only thing in the whole entire world that is wrong with Megan Jackson. She's pretty, she's nice, she's smart, she's athletic, she's friendly to dorks and others less fortunate than she is—she's just an all-around kind of amazing person.

And I thought this even *before* she decided to save my life.

I mean, I haven't always been crazy about her boyfriends, and occasionally she hijacks the bathroom, but basically, I scored big time with my big sister.

She's what they call "good people."

(I love that expression. How can a person be a "people"? What does it even mean?)

Charlie Joe's Tip #13

YOU CAN GO TO THE MOVIES AND STILL BE READING.

I love going to the movies. (When I'm not grounded, that is.) It's like one of my favorite things. And sometimes, when I get back from a movie and my parents ask me where I was, I say, "reading."

If I'm lyin' I'm dyin'.

Seriously. Check out all the ways you read at the movies:

1. *Ticket stub (Make sure you got a ticket for the right movie!)*
2. *Trailer credits*
3. *"This movie is rated . . ."*
4. *Opening credits*
5. *Subtitles (foreign movies can be good, and the girls are totally beautiful)*
6. *Closing credits*
7. *The posters outside the theater*
8. *The menu at the diner after the movie*

9. *The IMDB reviews of the movie that you check out when you get home*
10. *The texts you get from your friends arguing about whether the movie was any good or not*

So, after inwardly jumping up and down and screaming for joy—it was the library after all, and I didn't want to make a scene and distract all those dedicated readers—I decided to take my sister out for ice cream. It was the least I could do, and I kind of figured I owed her one, you know? (Actually, if you count the number of pages in *Billy's Bargain*, I owed her 167.)

So—and here is where the story gets weird—we get to the ice-cream place and who's there? *Timmy McGibney*. That's right—the backstabbing, book-plot-admitting, he's-in-as-much-trouble-as-you-are, supposedly grounded Timmy McGibney.

But it's not just that he was out when he was supposed to be in. After all, I'm also out when I'm supposed to be in.

It's who he's out with, who he's currently sharing a chocolate shake with . . . who he's breaking my heart with.

(Remember when I said that Timmy wasn't interested in girls yet? Well, scratch that.)

Drum roll, please. . . .

Say hello to Hannah Spivero.

You're probably wondering why I waited this long to introduce you to the love of my life.

Perfectly valid question.

To be honest, I wasn't sure I wanted to bring her up at all. I mean come on, what does Hannah Spivero have to do with this book? What does the most perfect creature that God and/or the universe ever created have to do with telling people how to not read?

As far as I can tell, nothing. So my intention was to leave her out of it—out of sight, out of mind, right?

Wrong.

I've been head over heels for Hannah Spivero since . . . what's today, Saturday? Let's see . . . Wednesday . . . Thursday . . . Friday . . .

About seven years.

I first laid eyes on Hannah in kindergarten, when she came up to bat in a kickball game. I was pitching. (Well, to be technical, rolling.) I was sporting that classic who-does-this-girl-think-she-is smirk as I gently guided the ball down the path to meet her girlishly uncoordinated foot.

Well, she pretty much kicked that ball to Arkansas. I think it's still going.

As she rounded first base, she stuck her tongue out at me.

As she rounded second base, she put her thumb on her nose and waggled her fingers at me.

As she rounded third base, she wrinkled her nose at me and smiled.

By the time she touched home plate, I was in love.

HANNAH SPIVERO

* * *

A BRIEF TRIBUTE TO HANNAH SPIVERO

Hannah's really smart, but not scary genius smart. She's not the most creative person, or the most funny, or the most anything, really. It's just that, well, for me, she's the most *everything*. No one else even comes close, as far as I'm concerned.

Here's an example. If you compare Hannah to Eliza (okay, I can hear my mother's voice saying "that's not a nice thing to do"), Eliza is definitely prettier piece by piece, if you get what I mean. Great hair, great eyes, great skin, great everything, and flirty in a way that says, "I'm gorgeous" over and over again to every guy she talks to.

Hannah, on the other hand, has black hair, perfectly pleasant eyes, and a tiny gap between her two front teeth that her braces never fixed. She loves life, she's always just totally herself, and she doesn't feel she has to broadcast to the world how pretty she is.

Plus she loves dogs, chocolate, and The Beatles, my three favorite things in the world.

The only downside to Hannah was her twin brother, Teddy. If Hannah is flawless, then Teddy is . . . well, flawful. He's always known that I'm in love with his sister and he's made it his mission in life to make me miserable.

But other than that, it was no contest. Piece by piece, Eliza is absolutely prettier, girlier, flirtier, that kind of thing. But when it comes right down to it, she's no Hannah.

Okay, enough obsessing.

But wait.

Here she was, sharing a shake with Timmy.

And it wasn't just that.

And it wasn't just that they were giggling, or that I could have sworn that his left pinkie was suspiciously close to her right index finger.

It was that they were sitting there, enjoying themselves, with what seemed like half the kids in my grade looking at them with awe and reverence. (Okay, it was probably only about ten kids, but you get what I'm saying.) Hannah wasn't wearing anything fancy—a "Let It Be" T-shirt and black jeans—but man, she looked good.

"Isn't that Hannah Spivero?" Megan asked, master of the obvious.

"Duh," I answered.

"What's she doing here with Timmy McGibney?" she asked, master of the obviously impossible-to-answer question.

"How am I supposed to know?" I said.

Before she could ask yet another irritating question, I headed straight for their table.

Timmy saw me coming and didn't seem the slightest

bit disturbed. In fact, he had a little gleam in his eye, like he was up to something.

"Hey, Charlie Joe. What are you doing here? Aren't you grounded?"

"Of course I'm grounded. Aren't you grounded?"

Timmy took a deep sip of his shake, which, I had to admit, looked completely delicious.

"I'm here with Hannah because we're studying together for the science test." It was a well-known fact that Hannah, on top of her countless other attributes and state of complete perfection, was extremely good at science.

I looked longingly at the many flavors of ice cream that waited, tantalizing, just out of reach. "Why do you get to go out for ice cream to study for science? Can't you do that at your house?"

It was here that Hannah decided to weigh in.

"Charlie Joe, did you get my text?"

This was totally off topic. She sent random texts to me all the time. They were always about annoyingly pointless topics, like what time the band concert was or when the Spanish homework was due. (Basically, any text from Hannah that didn't profess undying love was pointless.)

I turned to look at her, which as usual hurt my eyes a little bit. It's not like Hannah's beauty is blinding or anything; it's not. But she's got this glowing thing, like she swallowed a giant light bulb or something, and when I look at her I have to squint my eyes. Although I try to make sure no one notices.

"No, I didn't get your text. My parents took my cell phone away."

"Ouch," she giggled.

Timmy butted back in before Hannah and I got into anything resembling a conversation.

"Tryouts were pretty fun today, huh," he said, gloatingly.

"Yeah, they were super," I replied, sarcastically.

The lacrosse tryouts had been that morning. I didn't exactly set the place on fire. It was pretty obvious that Timmy was going to make the lacrosse team and I wasn't.

And, of course, Eliza had nothing to do with it.

Meaning, if Timmy hadn't been so insecure, and I hadn't been such a loudmouth buttinsky, we'd still be friends, he'd still be reading my books, and I wouldn't be sitting here watching him go straw to straw with my future wife!

Timmy took another long, luxurious sip of his shake, then looked at me. "You never answered my question. If you're grounded, why are you out getting ice cream?"

"Well, it just so happens Megan and me were at the library reading, thank you very much," I said.

"Megan and *I*," Hannah interrupted. It was another well-known fact that Hannah, on top of her countless other attributes and state of complete faultlessness, was also extremely good at grammar.

"Megan and *I*," I repeated for her benefit.

Timmy raised his eyebrows skeptically. "You were reading? Gimme a break." He dismissed me with a wave of his hand and returned to his shake.

For some reason I didn't stop there. "That's right. Not only was I reading, I finished *Billy's Bargain*. And I'll have you know it rocked."

Timmy raised his eyebrows farther than I thought was humanly possible. "You finished it? In one day?"

I was in too deep now. There was no retreat. "Pretty much." I started squirming in my mind a little bit.

"Really? What happens in the end?"

Before I could make up some sort of answer, Megan plopped down next to Hannah, as if they'd always been best friends. "I really like your shoes," she said, saving the day yet again.

Hannah looked at my sister in awe. She may have been a goddess in my eyes, but I guess deep down Hannah was just another middle school kid who got really excited when a high school kid paid attention to her.

As the two girls started gabbing about footwear, I saw my opening. "Well, I'm gonna go get us a couple of cones."

Timmy looked at me for a minute, then decided to go in for the kill.

"You know what, though? When I'm not grounded anymore, Hannah and me are going to go to the movies. We're going out now."

I stopped in my tracks. I started sweating. I saw my life flash before my eyes. (Sadly, a lot of it seemed to involve me adoring Hannah, and Hannah not particularly caring.) But mainly I was just completely shocked.

Hannah looked up from her conversation with Megan, and I could tell she was about to say something.

Thank God, she was going to put an end to this madness, and tell Timmy that that was the most ridiculous thing she'd ever heard.

But all she said was, "Hannah and *I*."

The chapters are getting longer.

I don't know what's happening. I'm trying to stop it, but it feels like it's out of my control a little bit.

I don't blame you if you're pretty mad at me right about now. I promised you very, very short chapters, and I'm not delivering.

I guess all I can say is that your customer complaints are duly noted, I'm aware of the problem, and I hope to have the system running normally again as soon as possible.

Thank you for your patience.

There, that's better.

Charlie Joe's Tip #14

IF YOU'RE FORCED TO READ A BOOK, MAKE
SURE YOU DON'T CARE ABOUT WHAT HAP-
PENS.

To make sure you don't get too invested in the
characters or story of whatever book you're
reading, please remember these simple facts:

1. *The characters aren't real. (fiction)*
2. *You don't know these people personally.
   (nonfiction)*
3. *They may well be dead. (historical
   biography)*
4. *They would ignore you in a restaurant.
   (sports biography)*
5. *What they're doing could never happen.
   (science fiction)*
6. *There's no way that awesome girl would
   fall in love with that dorky guy. (teen
   fiction)*
7. *There's no way that skinny kid could
   strike out that huge kid. (sports fiction)*

8. *None of this will matter later in life.*
   (math textbook)
9. *None of this will matter ever. (science*
   textbook)
10. *Who cares? (pretty much any book ever)*

The town I live in, Eastport, is one of those towns that's often called "a great place to raise kids."

I think the translation of that is "You kids have been given good schools, good teachers, good parents, good extracurricular activities, good sports teams, good arts programs, good tutors, and good guidance counselors. You kids have been given many things, and so the least you can do is take advantage of your good fortune and become extremely successful."

Not to put any pressure on us or anything.

But, hey, I'm not complaining. We have an awesome beach, a pretty cool downtown, a couple of movie theaters, and an amazing place called Jookie's (no one seems to know who or what Jookie is or was). Jookie's is an adult-free, stress-free zone where you can play Ping-Pong, shoot hoops, listen to music, and generally not have to think about parents or grades or anything important.

After the whole craziness at the ice-cream place, my sister and I went to Jookie's to recover.

I decided we should play air hockey, which is a great activity if you don't feel like talking, since it's too loud to have a conversation.

Megan tried anyway.

"THAT WAS WEIRD, HUH!" she shouted at me as she smacked the little red puck.

"YEAH!" I shouted, as I smacked back.

"YOU MUST BE REALLY ANNOYED RIGHT ABOUT NOW!" Megan concluded as she scored the winning goal, and both the game and the conversation were over.

Charlie Joe's Tip #15

MAKE SURE YOU'VE READ AT LEAST ONE BOOK TO COMPLETION, SO THAT IF SOMEONE ASKS YOU WHAT'S YOUR FAVORITE BOOK, YOU CAN ANSWER THE QUESTION.

I think the only book I ever read all the way through was *The Giving Tree.*

Have you ever read that? Man, that Shel Silverstein—one scary looking dude by the way, check out the picture on the back of the book—knew exactly how to write for non-readers like myself.

I think the whole thing had like sixty-two words at the most.

And yet it told the coolest story, about this little boy and his special friendship with this tree, and how the kid takes and takes and takes from the tree until the tree has nothing left to give. Eventually it's just a stump, and when the little boy comes back as an old man, a stump is all he needs, because he just needs a place to sit. Actually, as I describe it, it sounds kind of sad, but it's great. It's—well, I believe the word is *touching.*

Just between you and me? I have to admit I did cry a little bit there at the end.

It's almost enough to make someone want to read another book.

But not quite.

That night, as I was sitting in my room trying not to think about Timmy and Hannah, Megan knocked on my door. She came in before I could answer.

"How about that Timmy and Hannah," she said, plopping down on my bed.

I pretended not to care. "Yeah, whatever."

"So I started *Billy's Bargain*—it's actually really good," Megan went on, mercifully changing the subject. "The kid, Billy, goes through these ups and downs with the whole baseball thing, and by the end, when he's pitching in the big game, I was so nervous it was like I was actually there!" She looked me in the eye. "I would think a kid like you who enjoys sports would really go for a book like this."

"Yeah, well I like *playing* sports, not reading about them," I said.

She got up to go. "I know, I know," she said, giving me a sisterly smack on the shoulder—the kind that doesn't hurt at all. "All I'm saying is, one day you might find yourself on the pitcher's mound yourself, in a similar situation, and remembering how Billy dealt with it could actually help *you* deal with it."

That's adorable.

I waved what I hoped was a good-bye wave, but she just stood there in the doorway.

"You have to start reading sometime, you know," she said, lingeringly. "What are you going to do when the Position Paper comes up?"

I froze. The Position Paper was the huge assignment we had to do at the end of the year, and it involved a ton of books. Even though it was still a couple of months away, the thought of it already made me break out in a cold sweat.

I tried to shrug it off. "Why would you want to bring that up right in the middle of this wonderful brother-sister bonding moment?"

"I'm just saying," she said, but she decided not to push it.

"Thanks for reading the book, Megan," I said, meaning it.

"No sweat," she answered, also meaning it. "I'll write up a detailed synopsis tomorrow after I finish the book, if you need it."

"Oh, I need it," I said. She flicked my earlobe and walked out the door.

The next week went by like a blur—if blurs take about a thousand years and move at the speed of a glacier, that is. Here's a quick run-through.

Sunday: Megan totally comes through for me. Turns out she finishes *Billy's Bargain* in about two hours—how does she do it?—and she gives me an awesome synopsis of the book. I start to write my paper, which is due Friday, because I want to get it over with. But it's impossible to concentrate because I don't have my cell phone to text my friends and my dad had also disconnected the wireless on my laptop, so IM-ing wasn't an option either.

Adults don't get it, but us kids NEED to be doing seven other things while we're doing our homework. Otherwise we're so focused on the work that we can't focus on the work.

So it took me about five hours to write a paper that normally would've taken me two hours. But I finished the stupid thing and now I wouldn't have to think about it for a whole week.

NOTE TO PARENTS: Our academic, social, and future economic success depends on us being able to text,

IM, check Facebook, and call our friends every fifteen seconds while writing a school paper. Preferably while also playing "Call of Duty" at the same time.

If you want us to be able to concentrate, don't take away our distractions.

Monday morning: I get to school and I'm greeted by the sight of Eliza Collins running up to me like she just won the lottery.

"Did you hear Hannah Spivero and Timmy McGibney are going out?!"

I nod and walk maybe two more feet before Jake Katz runs up to me like he owns half of Eliza's winning lottery ticket.

"Did you hear Hannah Spivero and Timmy McGibney are going out?!?!"

Another nod, another two feet, and Pete Milano walks up to me and jabs me painfully in the ribs.

"Holy moly. Hannah Spivero and Timmy McGibney!"

Wait, is it too late to call in sick?

Monday afternoon: The whole school is getting a huge kick out of watching me watch Timmy and Hannah sit together at lunch.

The only one who shows any sympathy at all is Katie Friedman.

"Men," she said with a sigh, as we were putting our lunch trays away. It's a well-known fact that Katie is suspicious and quick to judge when it comes to the male sex.

"Women," I answered.

She laughed. "Are you okay?"

To anybody else, I would have lied.

To Katie, I said, "Not really."

She took my hand for just a second, then dropped it. Then she said, "Did you know that the average life span of a middle-school romance is nine days?"

Katie Friedman is a good person. She deserved a smile, so I tried to give her one.

"Only seven more days to go," I said.

Tuesday afternoon: In English class, things are looking up. It appears that Ms. Ferrell hasn't found out about the little arrangement that Timmy and I had. Then, at the end of class, she asks to see my paper, even though it's not due for another three days.

A bead of sweat pops out on my forehead. "But it's not due for another three days."

"I know that, Charlie Joe. I just want to see where you're at."

"But I've barely started it."

I was finished with the paper, of course, but she didn't need to know that. Especially since I had told her last Friday that I was "pretty much halfway through the book," which everybody knows translates to "I haven't exactly started it yet."

If I show her my final paper, she'll certainly wonder how the heck I managed to turn into a speed-reader.

I sneak a peak at Timmy, who's in the back row doodling in his notebook and enjoying the festivities, and suddenly I have a brainstorm: the truth.

"Actually, it's on my computer at home."

She hands me her cell phone. "Have your mom bring it in after school so we can go over it together."

Just my luck that my mom has her PTA meeting every Tuesday afternoon in the teacher's lounge.

Why does my mom have to be so caring and involved? Why can't she be more like one of those moms on the news who leaves her kids at the mall overnight?

I gulp. "Okay."

Timmy snickers and holds up his doodle: a picture of me lying in Moose's doghouse.

Tuesday, late afternoon: Things are no longer looking up. In fact, they're looking down.

On my way to meet my mom in the office, I get stopped by Mr. Radonski, a former school bully who found the perfect job—gym teacher.

"JACKSON!" No first names for this guy.

"Yes, Mr. Radonski?"

"If I catch you ONE MORE TIME with the wrong gym shorts on, I'm going to make you do push-ups till you bleed."

"Good to know, Mr. Radonski."

"JACKSON!!!"

"Yes, Mr. Radonski?"

"Stop being a WISEACRE."

"I'll stop being a wiseacre if you stop using words like *wiseacre*." (I don't say this, but I want to.)

He finally releases me, and I get the paper from my mom. From there I proceed immediately to the boys' room, where I throw out the third, fourth, and fifth pages, saving the first two.

I go to Ms. Ferrell's classroom, where I walk in on her crying on the phone.

She sees me and hangs up.

"Oh, Charlie Joe. Misty has a bloated stomach, and I'm not sure what's going to happen." Misty is her beloved Great Dane; there are pictures of her all over the classroom.

"A bloated stomach? Is that bad?"

She wipes her eyes with a tissue. "It can be."

Through my sympathy I see an opening. "Maybe we should do this another time."

"No, let's do this now," she sniffles. "It will help take my mind off it. Show me what you've got."

I give her my two pages. "If you don't mind my asking,

Ms. Ferrell, why do you want to see my paper before everyone else's?"

She wipes her eyes and looks at me for what seems like six days.

"Because, Charlie Joe, for some crazy reason I like you. I want you to do well. I want you to do great things, but for some reason you seem to want to do only okay things. Nothing more, nothing less. You seem to have no idea how bright you are, how"—and here her voice gets that tone adults use that makes you feel guiltier than ever—"*special*."

She sits down in her chair with a sigh. "If a teacher can get a student like you to fulfill his potential, she can retire happy." She sighs again. "And so I've decided to make you my project."

As we go over my two pages, word for word, for the next hour, I realize that when it comes right down to it, Ms. Ferrell is a pretty darn good teacher. Then she gets another call from the vet saying Misty is going to be okay, as long as she watches what she eats, and the next thing you know Ms. Ferrell gets so excited she flies out the door without even saying good-bye.

I may be her pet project, but I'm certainly not her pet Great Dane.

Wednesday: I plead for my cell phone back. Dad laughs. I plead louder. He laughs harder.

Thursday: Two *teachers* ask me if I've heard about Timmy and Hannah. Don't they have anything better to do?

Friday: Coco eats something bad and poops in the TV room. I get elected to clean it up. I turn in my paper. The two events are unrelated.

The weekend: Grounded, no phone, no Internet, no television, no life. It's so quiet and boring that not only could I hear the grass grow, I could hear it complain that it wasn't being watered enough. I develop a new respect for the Amish. (You know the Amish, right? They live in Pennsylvania and deny themselves basic necessities like cars, electricity, and Game Boy.)

Forty-eight hours feels like forty-eight years.

Things finally started looking up again on Monday.

Billy's Bargain was behind me. I wore the right shorts in gym class. Ms. Ferrell was in a great mood because her dog Misty was all better, ready to once again eat a small country.

And Hannah had a tiny pimple on her forehead.

Maybe the gods were smiling down on me after all.

At lunch, I looked for Timmy. I was feeling like it was time for a new start, and I decided to let bygones be bygones. I wanted to be the bigger man.

After all, Timmy was one of my oldest friends, and what's a little telling-his-mother-on-me-while-stabbing-me-in-the-heart between friends?

* * *

Timmy had come a long way since acquiring his

new lady friend, so it wasn't going to be easy squeezing into his table.

I believe the expression for what he was doing is "holding court"—telling his new admirers for the zillionth time about the exciting, nerve-racking moment when he finally got up the guts to ask Hannah out, never expecting in a million years that she'd say YES!

When he got to the end of this very inspirational story, his new best friends practically applauded in appreciation.

I felt a sudden wave of nausea.

Maybe I didn't want to be the bigger man after all. Maybe I wanted to be the smaller man. But I sucked it up and sat down.

Timmy saw me take a seat and called me over, like he was the new emperor, and I was some guy from the previous regime who was going to get one last delicious meal before being executed.

"Yo yo yo, if it ain't Charlie Joe!"

Timmy's new BFFs laughed as if Timmy were Dr. Seuss himself.

I handed him an ice-cream sandwich. "Here."

He looked a little confused. "What's this?"

"A peace offering."

A shocking left turn! Timmy's pals suddenly looked at me with something approaching respect. Maybe in good conscience they wouldn't be able to execute me after all. I guess there's something about doing the right thing that appeals to the savage beast in all of us.

Timmy quickly realized there was no choice but to accept the gift in the spirit in which it was given. "Um, thanks," he said, eloquently.

"You're welcome," I said, equally eloquently.

✷✷✷

We shook hands, and as he was delicately unwrapping the ice-cream sandwich, I leaned over and whispered, "You know, after we let a little time go by, and things get back to normal, there's no reason why we can't pick up our little arrangement just like before."

Timmy looked at me like I'd just smashed his lacrosse stick. "Are you crazy?" he hissed. "Do you want to spend the rest of your life at military school? I don't."

Uh-oh. The old arrangement was officially dead. Which meant I would have to figure out a new plan sooner rather than later.

The Position Paper was coming up.

It's just about halftime. Bring on the marching bands.

(Have I told you that Hannah can twirl a baton? She's awesome at it.)

Part Three
IF AT FIRST YOU NEVER READ, DON'T TRY AGAIN

Before we begin the next part of our story, it would probably help to understand exactly where my deep-seated love of not reading comes from.

It will help explain a lot.

I trace it back to a very specific, traumatic reading experience I had as a child.

I'll tell you all about it in the next chapter.

I think it was my sixth birthday. (I've tried to block it out, so some of the details are fuzzy.)

My dad, who's read about a zillion books—in my case, the apple not only fell far from the tree, it fell in another orchard, in another country—somehow got it in his mind that I was going to be the next great American writer.

I think maybe it had something to do with the fact that he had wanted to be a writer himself, but ended up a lawyer. "Hey, at least I get to write briefs," he says sometimes, although I'm not exactly sure what briefs are. In any event, he was dead certain I had the makings of a natural-born writer. I just needed to tap into my inner talent, let my imagination rip, and look out! All those boy wizards and six-pack-abs vampires would be running for the hills.

But according to Dad's master plan, before becoming the next great American writer, I had to become the next great American reader.

So I'm a typical about-to-be-six-year-old. I've spent approximately eleven months preparing for my birthday, including a failed attempt at getting people to give me presents on my half birthday, until at last the big day comes.

To say I'm excited is like saying Einstein knew addition.

Visions of trampolines and baseball bats are dancing in my head, and I'm running around the house screaming, "It's my birthday! It's my birthday! It's my birthday!"

All of a sudden my dad comes through the door, bursting with packages.

It's my birthday!

As I ran up to him, tons of presents spill out of the bags. I start to rip one open, and my dad says, "Not yet Charlie Joe! Let's gather the whole family."

You can pretty much guess the rest.

In front of my whole family, including Moose (we didn't have Coco yet), I proceed to rip open book after book after book—the entire works of Mark Twain, the entire works of Roald Dahl, and the entire works of Matt Christopher.

Now, nothing against those guys, but as far as I know none of them have ever played in the major leagues. Or built a trampoline.

Or even owned a trampoline.

After opening the last book, I did what any self-respecting brand-new six-year-old would've done.

I burst into tears and ran to my room.

To this day, whenever I hear the name Mark Twain, I burst into tears and run to my room.

P.S. I should clarify. When I said "traumatic reading experience," I should have said "traumatic near-reading experience."

I believe "traumatic reading experience" is what they call *redundant*.

So where were we?

During the next month or so, a lot happened.

Timmy and Hannah broke up, after nine days exactly (Thank you, Katie "Never Wrong" Friedman). Turns out that Hannah, sweetheart that she is, went out with Timmy to help him save face after the Eliza/lacrosse episode. I guess she figured that after nine days, his reputation was fully restored.

As a direct result of their breakup, I noticed I didn't feel that empty pit in my stomach/lungs/liver/heart area quite as much.

Eliza, meanwhile, was now going out with Ricky Summers, whose long, spectacular blond hair somehow made up for the fact that he was born without a personality.

And Katie was still my unofficial best friend, even though she was getting a little weirder by the day. First she made a random reference to becoming a nun—highly doubtful considering she's Jewish—which she then admitted was merely her way of saying that there were no good men in the world. Then she announced that with the right psychotherapy, even the most dysfunctional, out-of-it guy could be turned into the perfect boyfriend, and she would be just the girl to do it.

Jake Katz discovered some Web site where a woman read a different entire book every day for a year, and decided that someday he wanted to do that. (Kill me now.)

Ms. Ferrell brought Misty in on Bring Your Pet to School Day, which apparently only applied to her. She proceeded to eat the dry-erase board. (Misty, not Ms. Ferrell.)

As for me, I got a B+ on my *Billy's Bargain* paper. (Ms. Ferrell's note at the end: "It's a start.")

I got my cell phone back.

I got my computer back.

I got my mojo back.

It's always a little risky when I get my mojo back.

Charlie Joe's Tip #16

SPORTS ARE JUST AS EDUCATIONAL AS READING.

Think about it, there are tons of important lessons that you can learn on the field of play:

1. *Keeping score (math)*
2. *Being part of a team (social studies)*
3. *Learning how to throw a curve ball (physics)*
4. *"2-4-6-8, who do we appreciate?" (poetry)*
5. *Knowing your batting average, or completion percentage, or shooting percentage (statistics, which apparently is a type of math)*

About a week later, on a particularly fine spring morning, me and my mojo found ourselves on the pitcher's mound for my travel baseball team. We were good, not great—all the elite players having been snatched up by the fancy, ridiculously expensive, year-round "premiere" baseball programs. (In youth sports these days, the best athletes play one sport all year long, almost like a job. It's crazy.) But the grass was green, the sky was blue, the bases were white, and it was a good day to play ball.

My parents were there, and of course they'd brought the dogs. (Moose and Coco were huge baseball fans, mainly because of the dropped hot dog scraps.)

We were up, 4–3, going into the last inning. So I was channeling my inner Mariano Rivera, trying to put the thing away for my team, but after two quick outs I walked their number nine hitter, Jeff Kleiner, who hasn't taken the bat off his shoulder all season. (I always walk those kids for some reason. You know how the coach always says, "Throw it, don't aim it?" Easier said than done.)

Then, up comes their leadoff hitter, this short but incredibly fast kid named Andrew.

"Strike him out!" my dad hollered.

"Hit one out!" his dad hollered.

"Pipe down before we kick you both out," both moms whispered.

So I'm standing on the mound, trying to stare down Andrew, and I start thinking about glory. Okay fine, not "premiere team" glory, but good solid travel team glory. I start thinking about how much I want to strike this kid out, and how I would give anything to be able to do it.

Which rang a really distant bell somewhere in my head. Who was it that said he'd give anything to win his baseball game? Someone I know, some other pitcher . . . but I couldn't remember who it was.

I'm twirling the baseball in my hand, staring in at speedy little Andrew, when it suddenly occurs to me.

I realize the person I'm trying to remember is Billy.

That's right. *Billy's Bargain* Billy.

Yikes.

* * *

Wow. Okay. So THIS was what it was like to identify with a character in a book.

It was true. I started thinking about Billy like he was a real person. What would Billy do in this situation? Would he have the confidence to get this final out? Or would all his doubts and fears come back to haunt him, and make him choke?

Would Billy be the hero and get carried off the field on the shoulders of his teammates, or would he be the goat, and wind up alone at 7-Eleven, drowning his sorrows in a Big Gulp?

Then I remembered my conversation with my sister Megan, when she predicted this exact thing would happen. Dang her! Why do people like my sister and Katie always have to be so right all the time?

Now remember, I'd only read the first and last chapters, but all of a sudden I was acting like a . . . wait for it . . . *reader*. I was thinking about the book and, even more to the point, I was remembering what happened in it, and—my heart sank—I *cared* about what happened.

What was happening to me?

I'm not going to lie; I was scared.

I shuddered, then snapped back to reality. I still had

Andrew to contend with. After shaking off the catcher's suggestions of a knuckleball and a curve—mainly because, as we both knew, I didn't know how to throw either one—I wound up and fired my best fastball.

"THWACK!"

Andrew scorched one that looked like it was heading to the right-center field gap—with his speed, a certain inside-the-park, game-winning homer.

But wait! There, out of nowhere, comes a blur. It's none other than right fielder and relentless reader Jake Katz, who had somehow managed to stop dreaming about books long enough to race to the ball . . . adjust his glasses . . . track it down . . . and make an incredible, diving, game-saving catch!

Holy moly!!!

Needless to say, it was Jake who had his *Billy's Bargain* moment. He was carried off the field, not me. I was neither the hero nor the goat.

I was just a lucky kid who had dodged two bullets: the baseball and the book.

Charlie Joe's Tip #17

READING MAKES YOU BLIND.

Show me a kid with straight A's, and I'll show you a kid with glasses.

No, seriously. Maybe not 100 percent of the time, but definitely at least 90, the smart kids are the ones with the bad eyes.

The reason? Simple. Too many small words on a page.

You don't have to be an optometrist to know that a person who uses his eyes too much will wear them out faster than someone who uses his eyes for less challenging activities—say, for example, closing them during science class.

Take it from this 20/20 guy, if you don't want to be called "four eyes," forget the books.

Meanwhile, there were only six weeks left in the school year.

Which meant one thing: those dreaded two words that no kid at my school ever wants to hear.

Position Paper.

The Position Paper is God's way of saying "before you get to enjoy the fruits of summer, you're going to have to suffer through some serious homework."

Basically it involves picking a topic—capital punishment, say, or child obesity, or smoking in movies—doing a ton of research (which involves reading a ton of BOOKS), and presenting a six-page paper OUT LOUD, IN CLASS to ALL THE TEACHERS IN THE ENGLISH DEPART-MENT.

I know, right? Talk about capital punishment.

It was obvious that my *Billy's Bargain* moment on the pitcher's mound, combined with the impending doom of the Position Paper, made the situation a full-fledged emer-gency.

So naturally, on the night before the deadline for pick-ing a topic, I was in Megan's room, lying on her bed with her stuffed animals (what is it with girls and stuffed animals?), begging for help.

"I warned you about the Position Paper," was the first thing she said. "You didn't listen."

She didn't really lift my spirits when she told me that writing her Position Paper was the hardest thing she ever had to do in her life—beating out the other hardest thing she ever had to do in her life, which involved telling the 260-pound, slightly insane captain of the high school football team that despite his driving all over our front lawn to prove his love, she *still* didn't want to go out with him.

As I sat there tossing one of her teddy bears up and down, getting more and more nervous, I told her about the frightening *Billy's Bargain* episode on the baseball field.

All she said to that was, "Jake Katz saved the game? That's awesome!"

Then I noticed a book lying on her desk: *Cliques And Doubleclicks*.

As much as I disliked books, I had to admit that was a pretty interesting title.

"What's that book about?" I asked Megan.

She threw it to me. "Read it and find out."

"No, seriously."

She grabbed it back. "It's actually this really cool book about how cliques are bad for kids, how they're an epidemic in school, and how the Internet is just making it harder for teachers and guidance counselors to deal with them." She opened up her laptop. "I'm writing a paper about it."

Now typically, talk of textbooks and papers is my cue to leave, but all of a sudden a lightbulb went off in my head.

Cliques. Boys. Girls.

Hold on a minute.

Suddenly a beautiful, perfect, fully-formed plan materialized in my brain.

"I got it!" I shouted, throwing Megan's teddy bear onto the bed so hard that it knocked over her giraffe, her turtle, and two of her little penguins.

The next day, I found Timmy hanging out in the hall with a couple of kids who had decided to still be his friend even after Hannah broke up with him. (They probably figured she might change her mind, and they wanted to be there when he got her back.)

I called him over.

"Timmy, got a sec?"

"Sure."

I pulled him into an empty classroom so no one else could hear us.

"I want to run something by you."

"What?"

This wasn't going to be easy, but I had to be up front with Timmy, because I needed him on my side.

"We all know that you went out with Hannah to get back at me."

Timmy was offended. "That's crazy!"

"And Hannah went out with you because she felt bad for you," I added.

This time Timmy just looked at his shoes.

"You know it's true," I insisted. "That's how she rolls.

She's not like the rest of us. She likes to do nice things, and she doesn't care about what other people think."

Timmy thought about it. He was a pretty well-liked kid, but he knew that he wasn't really in Hannah's league. A feeling I knew all too well.

"Come on, that's what's so great about her," I added.

Timmy sighed, and he didn't have to say anything. I could tell that he wasn't about to argue with me.

"So what's your point," he said instead.

"I'm going to set up Jake and Hannah."

You know that expression "his eyes bugged out of his head"? I'd always thought that was a ridiculous exaggeration, until I saw Timmy at that moment.

"No way."

"Yes way."

"No WAY!!"

"Yes way."

Timmy took a deep breath. He'd had an up-and-down year, no doubt about it—king of the hill one second, back among the regular people the next—and this might be one roller-coaster ride too many.

"Why? Did Jake ask you to? Just because she went out with me, suddenly every guy thinks he has a chance?"

My turn to take a deep breath. "Actually, it was my idea."

Timmy was speechless. For about a second and a half. Then he said the only logical thing. "Why?"

"Because my Position Paper is going to be about why cliques are bad for kids. And if I can get the two of them to go out, it would prove that two kids from totally different worlds could ignore peer pressure and go out," I explained. (Actually, Hannah was the one who'd feel the peer pressure. Jake would feel nothing but claps on the back from his awed and amazed friends.)

"But isn't she still going out with James?" Timmy asked, looking to poke holes in my plan.

She was indeed. James was a one-man clique buster himself, one of those freaks of nature who managed to do drama club and play sports, and it somehow all worked. Girls LOVED him.

James and Hannah had been going out for about two weeks, well past Katie Friedman's nine-day expiration date, but there were rumors they were on the rocks.

"That won't last, trust me," I said.

He eyed me suspiciously, like he knew I was up to something.

"It feels like you're leaving something out," he said.

I'd known Timmy a long time. We'd been through a lot together.

I lowered my voice. "Well, here's the thing. You know that deal we used to have?"

Timmy licked his lips, clearly thinking about free ice-cream sandwiches. "Yeah?"

"Well, ever since we got caught, I've been trying to come up with a new plan."

He suddenly got where I was going, and just started shaking his head in disbelief. I pretended not to notice.

"Well anyway," I continued, "I figured Jake would be so happy going out with Hannah that he wouldn't mind just doing me one little favor."

Timmy knew the answer to the question he was about to ask, but he asked anyway. "What favor?"

"Reading all my books for the Position Paper."

Timmy didn't say anything, so I filled the silence. "Well? What do you think? Awesome, right?"

Timmy let out a whistle. "So let me get this straight," he said. "The girl you've had a crush on since kindergarten, the girl that made you so jealous when I went out with her that you couldn't sleep for two weeks, the girl that you plan on marrying some day, whether she agrees to it or not . . . you're going to set her up with Jake Katz just so you can get out of reading some books?"

Jeez, did he have to put it that way?

"Yeah," I answered.

He laughed and scratched his head. Suddenly I wondered what I would do if he told me it was a terrible idea.

But Timmy didn't think it was a terrible idea. In fact, he had a pretty good idea of his own.

"Instead of being sneaky about it, why don't you just tell them both that you're doing it for your paper? That way they could become part of your experiment, and they'd probably both get really into it," Timmy said.

I blinked. "You think?"

Timmy nodded. "Definitely. Hannah loves to surprise people. Like you said, she's not like the rest of us. I learned that early on in our relationship."

It occurred to me that Timmy's use of the word *relationship* to describe their brief moment in time together was a bit extreme, but why bring that up when he was being so supportive?

"I wouldn't exactly call it a relationship," I said.

Sometimes a guy just can't help himself.

Charlie Joe's Tip #18

IF YOU HAVE TO READ, READ ABOUT GIRLS. IT HELPS YOU UNDERSTAND THEM BETTER.

We all know how painful reading can be. So if you have to read, at least make sure you get something important out of it.

And learning how to deal with girls is important.

Therefore, you should only read books with lots of girls in them. It's a great way to learn about these mysterious, fascinating creatures.

(I should mention this tip is primarily for boys. I suppose for girls the reverse is true, but I wouldn't know.)

Katie Friedman had never worried about being popular, as long as she was popular.

Meaning she wasn't one to be concerned about being "in" with the "in kids," because she didn't really have an "in kid" personality. But all sorts of differents kinds of kids liked Katie, because she always had good insights into people's behavior, and was generous and not too judgmental. (Now that I think about it, she probably *will* make a good therapist someday.)

She did, however, have a hard-core group of friends she cared deeply about, a bunch of smarty-pants types who all shared the same interests—namely, a complete lack of interest in anything other people were interested in, and a total fascination with things nobody else even knew existed.

The day after my conversation with Timmy, I found Katie and her friends in the middle of a big discussion about why the original cast of the 1975 Broadway production of *Chicago*, starring Gwen Verdon and Chita Rivera, was way better than the original cast of the 1996 production of *Chicago*, starring Bebe Neuwirth and Anne Reinking, even though the revival was way more successful than the original.

The only reason I knew this on such a frighteningly detailed level was because I had heard this particular debate about seven thousand times. It was not information that I, nor any middle school kid, should ever need or want to have.

I knew that Chicago was where the Cubs played, and personally that was good enough for me.

Which was why I didn't feel the slightest bit guilty for interrupting rudely.

"Katie, I need to talk to you. NOW!"

Katie looked up from her tea—a beverage that middle school kids drink to look like high school kids, and high school kids drink to look like college kids—and, as usual, made me her priority.

The girl could give lessons in being a good friend.

"Over here," she said, walking to the Forbidden Zone. (In the old days, when our school was a high school, the Forbidden Zone was the smoking section of the cafeteria. It still had kind of a naughty, scary quality about it, so no one ever sat there.) She pulled up a chair and patted another one for me. "What sort of trouble has my favorite scoundrel gotten himself into now?"

I wasn't sure what she meant by *scoundrel*, but it had the word *favorite* attached to it, so I let it go.

"No trouble."

She laughed. "You don't come to me unless you're either in trouble, or you're hatching a plan. So spill."

I grinned. "Right. Like I said, no trouble."

A horrified look crossed her face. "Oh God. This is no time for one of your schemes. You need to be laying low and playing by the rules for the foreseeable future."

Did I mention that Katie was the one person in the world who knew absolutely everything about me? That I sucked my thumb until I was seven, that I was afraid of the dark until I was nine, that I was too scared to sleep over anyone's house until I was about, well, now, and that Timmy and I had had our books-for-ice-cream-sandwiches arrangement for two years until he ruined everything with the telling-on-me-then-dating-Hannah thing?

Katie knew all that. She even knew that the mere mention of Mark Twain could bring me to tears.

So obviously she knew what she was talking about when she told me I should stop what I was about to start.

Only as usual, I wasn't listening.

"So I want to set up Jake Katz and Hannah. Do you think she'll go for it? She likes to shock people, right?"

She looked at me.

"How clueless are you?" she asked. "Don't you remember what happened when you talked to Eliza about Timmy?"

"This is different," I said.

"Different how?" she asked.

"Don't worry, I'll explain later," I went on.

Katie sighed. She looked at me like she was on a cliff,

and I was the water, and she couldn't decide if she wanted to jump in or not.

"I don't want to know," she finally said.

I exhaled and spoke at the same time.

"My question is, do you think I need to give Hannah something to get her to do it? Like, what do you think I need to give her to make her go along with the plan?"

Katie thought about it for about eight seconds.

"She loves The Beatles, right? If you really want to be sure, give her one of your cool Beatles tchotchkes. That ought to do the trick," she said. (I think *tchotchkes* is a Jewish word, but don't quote me. And if I'm spelling it right, you can thank the computer.)

No questions. No judging. Just the right answer.

I hugged her, and as she walked back to her friends she looked back at me and said, "Just be careful."

That's why Katie Friedman is awesome.

✳ ✳ ✳

But the other part? The "I'll explain later" part, about me getting Jake to read my books?

I never did explain that to Katie.

And she didn't find out about it until it was too late.

The next day at lunch, Hannah Spivero was finishing the last of the three chocolate puddings she had every day for dessert (I told you she was perfect). I sat down next to her and cut to the chase.

"You and James broke up, right?"

She giggled. "Yup. He's amazing, but it didn't work out." I wasn't sure how that made sense, but I didn't have time to analyze it.

"Do you like anyone else?"

"Not at the moment. Why, are you interested?" she said.

I know, that sounds mean because of course she knew I was interested, but it wasn't. We always played this silly game, where she would flirt with me and I would never have the nerve to actually flirt back.

But this time was different. This was no time for games. I said, "I need you to do something for me."

She put down her pudding.

This was a side of me she'd never seen before. All business. Brisk and serious. Commanding even. Absolutely no pathetic-ness whatsoever.

"What is it, Uncle Charlie?"

Usually I wasn't crazy about it when people gave me

nicknames, like "Chaz" or "Chuck" or "Chuckles" or "C.J."
Why couldn't I be just plain old "Charlie Joe"? But when
Hannah came up with "Uncle Charlie," it sounded like the
most natural nickname in the world. Almost like music.
The most—

Dang it, I was getting distracted again.

I took her hand. (It's amazing how brave a desperate
man could be.) "I think you should go out with Jake Katz."

Her eyes narrowed in confusion. I was confusing her!
This was definitely a side benefit of my plan. Anytime I
caused Hannah to feel any kind of real emotion, it could
definitely be considered a triumph.

"Why would I do that?" she asked.

"Because if you do, you would have my undying love
forever," I answered, looking deeply into her glowing eyes.

"I have that already," she answered back, as if it were
the most obvious thing in the world. Which it was.

I remembered Katie's suggestion, and much as it pained
me, it was the only way. Hannah Spivero had broken my
heart long enough; it was time to break my own heart.

I sighed. "Okay listen. If you do this for me, you can
have my original limited-edition collectors' item "Dead
Babies" Beatles *Yesterday and Today* LP album cover," I
said mournfully.

Just a quick explanation: one time The Beatles put out
an album where the cover was a picture of them holding a
bunch of bloody baby parts, which became known as the

"Dead Babies" cover. Even though the babies were clearly fake, like dolls, people were still totally grossed out, and The Beatles had to change the cover immediately. As a result, there were barely any of the original covers printed, but I was lucky enough to own one—a birthday gift from my dad (who was still trying to make up for the Mark Twain disaster).

It was yet another element of Hannah's amazing-ness that she loved The Beatles as much as I did, and surely she would love owning this album cover *almost* as much as I did.

"Wow. You would actually part with that just to make people think that I like Jake Katz? I don't get it. I'm not interested in dating Jake Katz, so why would I suddenly agree to go out with him? No one would believe it anyway." She winked. "It's almost as crazy as people thinking I'm suddenly in love with *you*."

Ouch. That was a shot to the gut.

I soldiered on bravely, silently reminding myself that a truly great man fights on even when the odds are against him. "That's not necessarily true. I mean, I know, yeah, everyone knows I've always kind of had a thing for you ('Kind of had a thing?' Who was I kidding?), but it's possible that other kids could think that maybe deep down, you could like someone like me. Or Jake."

She giggled, and suddenly I felt the need to backtrack a bit. "I'm not saying it's true, not at all, but it's not like it's impossible, right?"

Hannah looked at me like she was looking into the future, like she was thinking, well, God knows I don't like this little puppy dog licking his paws right in front of me, but it's not out of the realm of human existence that maybe, someday down the road, I might find him reasonably attractive.

"I suppose not," she finally admitted, giving me a tiny sliver of my dignity back.

I suddenly remembered Timmy's advice to be up front about the reason. "I'm glad we got that out of the way," I announced. "So here's the thing. I'm writing my Position Paper on why cliques are bad for kids, and why it's important that we figure out a way to stop them. I want to show people that it's possible, and the best way to do that is for someone like you to go out with someone like Jake."

Hannah looked at me. I mean, *really* looked at me. Possibly for the first time since she stuck her tongue out at me seven years ago.

"That's interesting," she said.

Please mark the day and time—May 14, 11:44 a.m.—because, for the first and possibly only time in my life, Hannah Spivero found me, or at least something I said, interesting.

For that brief, shining moment, I had the upper hand. It felt fantastic.

But she quickly recovered. Moment over.

"Why didn't you say that in the first place?" she said. "That sounds like a cool project. I would have done it even without the awesome Beatles album cover."

Hannah Spivero had an uncanny ability to make you feel happy and sad in the same sentence.

"Deal," she said.

"Deal," I repeated.

For some weird reason I stuck out my hand and she shook it, like we were doing a business deal.

"The only thing is, you can't tell anybody why you're doing it until I present my paper," I said importantly.

"It'll be our little secret," said Hannah Spivero, winking. "Can I have my hand back now?"

Charlie Joe's Tip #19

IF YOU ABSOLUTELY, POSITIVELY HAVE TO READ A BOOK, MAKE SURE IT'S ON A TOPIC YOU LIKE.

If you are a boy, you probably like books about: sports, spies, superheroes, getting lost in the woods.

If you are a girl, you probably like books about: sensitive, hunky vampires with a weakness for brunettes.

If you are Jake Katz, you like: books with words in them.

Jake Katz is a really good guy, despite his love of books.

His mother, on the other hand, is really kind of annoying. She belongs in what my parents refer to as "the room."

Let me explain.

My parents invented "the room." It's an imaginary place where they put all the adults they know that never shut up about themselves, or their families, or their kids, and how amazing they all are, without ever taking a breath long enough to ask you anything about how you're doing.

My parents love the idea of all these incredibly self-absorbed people in one room, bragging on and on, no one listening to a word anyone else is saying because they're all too busy yakking about themselves.

Jake Katz's mom isn't just *in* "the room." She's a founding member.

Which is why my mom wasn't looking forward to taking me to Jake's house that Friday afternoon. She loved Jake—and thought he and his study habits were a good influence on me, of course—but she didn't exactly relish the idea of listening to Mrs. Katz blab on about their vacation house in Nantucket, her daughter's freshman year on the Brown University crew, her husband's promotion to chief executive in charge of making money, or just her family's general wonderfulness.

When we pulled up, I hopped right out of the car, so my mom could make a quick getaway. But as usual, Ms. Katz was already running out the door, yelling, "Claire, we have so much to talk about."

She was already mid-brag by the time she reached the driveway.

My mom rolled down the window and called me over. "It's like I have a sign on my forehead that says 'talk my ear off,'" she whispered. Then she got out of the car and greeted Mrs. Katz with a big smile. "How are things?" she said, warmly. That's how my mom rolls. She's a good one.

As Jake and I escaped up to his room, I could vaguely hear Mrs. Katz start to talk about the new Lexus SUV she was completely enamored of, and that the gas mileage was so much better than you might think, and my mom agreeing that yes, it was a terrific car.

* * *

A lot of nerds just like to talk about nerdy things, like science and Jar Jar Binks. Jake wasn't like that.

He liked to talk about girls. A lot.

But the cool thing about Jake was, he was never one of those kids who felt sorry for himself because he wasn't

Mr. Popular or anything. He still had a certain confidence about him. It was almost as if he realized that his time to shine would come later in life, and so he took everything that happened to him now in stride.

Right now he was playing computer scrabble and taking in stride the fact that he'd probably be going solo to the end-of-the-year dance.

"The thing I like about going by myself is the fact that I'm not going to feel like I have to stay with my date the whole night," he was saying. "If I feel like getting some punch, I can go get some punch. If I feel like hanging with my friends, I can hang with my friends. It's actually going to be a real advantage, not having to be tied down to one woman."

It was hard to change the subject with Jake when he was on a roll, but I had to give it a shot.

"Dude, that's still like a month away," I said. "There's a lot going on before that. Our Position Papers, for example."

"Oh, right." Talking about schoolwork bored Jake, probably because he was so unchallenged by it.

Still, I had an agenda to keep. "So anyway, mine's gonna be about cliques in school, and about why they exist, and if they're bad."

Jake snorted. "Of course they're bad. Cliques stink." He was passionate on the subject, for good reason.

"So, my plan is to show that cliques can be overcome, even eliminated, if only kids would give it a chance. And I want to prove it by giving an example of two people from very different cliques going out."

He looked at me. He was too smart not to know what I was up to.

"Who'd you have in mind?"

"Well, I was thinking you and Hannah." I held my breath.

He laughed. "That's crazy! I'm no idiot, Charlie Joe. I know the deal. I could set my mind to getting someone like Hannah, or any of the really popular girls, for about ten years, and I'm pretty sure it would never happen."

"Well, that's what's great about Hannah, she's not like all the other popular girls. She's different. And it just so happens I already talked to her about it and she's totally into it. She *wants* you to ask her out!"

"I bet she can't wait," Jake said.

"It's going to be so cool," I continued. "But here's the thing. We're not going to tell anyone it was my idea, so we can see how the school reacts. And then I can analyze it for my Position Paper."

Jake pondered this. "So, it's not that she likes me, it's that she's agreed to be part of a social experiment," he said, fully grasping the situation.

"Something like that," I admitted. "But my guess is, once she finds out what you're really like, she'll probably end up liking you anyway."

"You think so, really?" he asked.

Even though it seemed like a long shot, and the possibility scared me to death, for some reason I actually believed it.

"Really really," I answered.

Jake stared deeply into his computer, as if asking it for guidance. Finally he looked up at the ceiling. "Wow," he said. "Like, wow. Okay, let's do it."

"Now you're talking!" I said, smacking him on the back. "Come on, let's go out and shoot some hoops."

"Okay," he said, folding up his laptop. He seemed like he wasn't quite sure what had just happened. "Thanks, I think," he said.

"You guys are going to be awesome together," I said as we headed outside.

✳ ✳ ✳

We were halfway through our game of H-O-R-S-E— I was winning by one letter—when I casually brought up another subject, as if I had just thought of it.

"Oh dude, one more thing. Is it cool if you help me with some of the books I have to read for my Position Paper? Maybe you could just read them really quickly, since you read so fast and everything, and then kind of give me the lowdown on what's in them."

Jake was dribbling around with an extra spring in his step, already feeling Hannah's wind beneath his wings. It was hard to tell what he was thinking, so I decided to keep talking.

"The thing is, I got this list of books from my sister and it's totally brutal. They're so freakin' long and hard, and I'm totally nervous I'm not going to be ready."

Suddenly he looked at me and smiled the glorious, untroubled smile of a Hannah-dater. "No problem-o, my man. What are friends for?"

And then he came back and beat me, H-O-R-S-E to H-O-R-S.

So I'd talked to Timmy, Katie, Hannah, and Jake. They all thought it was a good plan and I was a genius. (Not including Katie.) The stage was set. The die was cast. The egg was ready to hatch.

I may not like to read, but I know a good metaphor when I see one.

Part Four

IT SEEMED LIKE A GOOD IDEA AT THE TIME

That Friday night at dinner, my mom asked me why I was in such a good mood.

"Because I'm going to a party tonight," I answered.

"Can you not eat like a dog?" she answered back, which didn't have to do with anything, except maybe for the fact that I was licking my plate at that particular moment.

"Mom doesn't mean just tonight," dad chimed in. "She means in general. You seem to be in a great mood, which is interesting considering you have your big paper coming up, and we all know how much you love schoolwork."

I knew what they were getting at. They didn't really want to know why I was happy. They wanted to know if I was up to my old tricks.

Megan, who was eating, texting, and combing her hair all at the same time, heard the word *schoolwork* and looked up.

"What are we talking about?"

"Why I'm happy," I said, helping myself to some more pasta.

My sister looked at my parents. "Come on you guys, give Charlie Joe a break," she said, bless her heart. "He's been working pretty hard lately, and he picked a really cool topic for his Position Paper."

"Oh?" said my mom. "What's it about?"

This could have gone one of two ways. I could have told them, which *definitely* would have led to at least fourteen more questions on the matter. Or I could have not told them, which *might* have led to fourteen more questions on the matter.

"I'd rather keep it a surprise," I said, which didn't really make any sense, now that I think about it.

My parents looked at each other, and decided to accept it. Or, at least for now, let it go.

"Well, I look forward to reading it," said my dad, who then proceeded to lick his own plate, much to my mom's horror.

"Do I live in a kennel?" she sputtered, before giving her plate to Moose and Coco so they wouldn't completely miss out.

Middle-school parties are all pretty much the same: cold pizza, soggy cookies, flat soda, deafening music, a couple of kids kissing, a ton of kids pretending not to look but actually staring at the kids kissing, and the little sister of the host constantly coming in and out, supposedly to see if the chips bowl needs refilling, but really just to check out what was going on and report back to the parents that nobody had overdosed on potato chips and was projectile vomiting on the couch.

That Friday night at Kelly Dunn's house, the stars of the show were Jake Katz and Hannah Spivero.

Jake had asked Hannah out at lunch two days earlier, and it took about eight minutes for the entire school to know. I guess a good way to describe the reaction was shock and awe.

Hannah's friends were shocked, and Jake's friends were awed.

Their first date was Kelly's party. You can pretty much imagine the reaction.

They weren't making out or anything, but they were doing something almost as shocking. They were talking and laughing. And while other people couldn't take their eyes off of them, it seemed like Jake and Hannah couldn't take their eyes off each other.

I realized I had never really seen either of them laugh and talk so much at the same time.

Naturally, I had mixed emotions.

I was delighted that my experiment was working so well.

And I was miserable that my experiment was working so well.

✳ ✳ ✳

The very idea that head cheerleader Hannah Spivero and head bookworm Jake Katz were hanging out at a party together was already too much for people to take.

But when they began to dance, the whole party ground to a halt.

At first, people stopped talking altogether and stared openmouthed. You could hear a pin drop. Then there was a new kind of buzz in the conversation, kind of a freaked-out whispering, lots of omigods, that kind of thing.

It took Kelly Dunn's little sister, who had come into the room on one of her periodic spying missions, to blurt out what everyone was thinking.

"Holy crap!" she said.

And it took Teddy Spivero—Hannah's obnoxious, annoying twin brother—to blurt out what *I* was thinking.

"Hey, Jackson, what happened? All those years panting after my sister and little Jake Katz gets her? But don't worry, maybe one day that will be you."

He took a deep swig of his punch. "Yeah, one day in the year TWO THOUSAND AND NEVER!" Everyone cracked up.

Even I had to admit, that was a pretty good one.

Charlie Joe's Tip #20

WHEN YOU'RE MORE THAN HALFWAY THROUGH A BOOK, PICK UP THE PACE, SKIM A BIT, AND GET IT OVER WITH AS QUICKLY AS POSSIBLE.

You know those people who finish a book and then say, "I'm so sad it's over"? I have news for them.

The person who wrote the book isn't sad it's over, otherwise he or she would have kept writing. In fact, it's the opposite. They're relieved. Thrilled. Ready to celebrate.

It should be the same for the reader. Finishing a book is cause for rejoicing, not regret.

So hurry up. You're more than halfway home. Pedal to the metal, people.

It's pretty much an unwritten rule that at every school assembly at every school in the nation, people sit with their own clique. Jocks sit with jocks, dorks sit with dorks, Chinese kids sit with Chinese kids, and so on.

But not at our school. Not anymore.

Because here's the thing: ever since Jake and Hannah started going out—and actually seemed to *like* each other— the whole rest of the school had slowly, carefully, warily started to stray from their cliques.

Listen, I'm not saying it was a social earthquake or anything. It was just a few small things here and there. Like the way people sat at school assemblies, for example.

At today's assembly, which happened to be about why the cafeteria had replaced all the good snacks that were bad for you with bad snacks that were good for you, Jake sat next to Hannah, who sat next to Jack Humphries (jock), who sat next to Mark Fricker (dork), who sat next to Lauren Hu (Chinese kid).

It was a beautiful thing to see.

✳ ✳ ✳

After the assembly, Ms. Ferrell was standing near the auditorium with Mr. Dormer and Ms. Axlerod—two social studies teachers whom everybody assumed were going out, just because they were the two best-looking teachers in the school.

I knew Dormer was good-looking because all the moms—including, I'm horrified to say, my own—would get all giggly whenever they saw him.

I knew Ms. Axelrod was good-looking because I have two eyes.

In any event, Ms. Ferrell saw me and called me over.

"Charlie Joe, why were all the kids sitting with different kids today? I've never seen that before in all my years at this school!"

"I know," I said. "Can you believe it?" I didn't want to get too far into the topic.

(For some reason, whenever Ms. Ferrell had an interesting observation to make about the student body—good or bad—she made it to me. Sometimes the observations were neither good nor bad, but just random. Like "Why are all the boys in this school so fascinated with skateboarding?" Or "What's with all the girls suddenly straightening their hair?" I guess she assumed I would care. Not a very accurate assumption.)

Mr. Dormer put his arm around me. "Mr. Jackson, I hear you're a very bright kid, but a bit of a slacker."

My first thought was why wasn't it Ms. Axlerod who was putting her arm around me?

My second thought was deny, deny, deny. "I wouldn't say that's true at all."

I tried to slip out of his grasp but he tightened his grip.

"Well, I hope to have you in my class one day," Mr. Dormer said, "because we'll find out once and for all." And then he whacked me playfully on the back. "In my class, the only one who's allowed to be a slacker is me!"

He roared at his own joke—an inexcusable violation of the comedy rulebook, if you ask me—and Ms. Axlerod fake laughed right along with him.

That clinched it. They were dating.

Oh Ms. Axelrod, how could you?

＊＊＊

Ms. Ferrell tried to regain control of the conversation.

"Anyway, Charlie Joe, what are your plans for the summer?"

Grateful for the change in topic, I launched into a long, detailed description of my summer agenda.

"Not much."

Mr. Dormer hijacked again.

"Ah to be in your shoes, Mr. Jackson," he said. "What I

wouldn't give to be a kid again. Except for the pimples and the Position Paper, of course!" He ended every attempted joke with the verbal equivalent of an exclamation point.

Did being handsome give him the right to be so completely not funny?

"Well, I gotta get to class," I said, trying to get away. "Don't want to be late and give anyone the idea that I'm a slacker."

Ms. Axlerod laughed at that—an actual, genuine laugh, which sounded nothing like her Dormer fake laugh.

Mr. Dormer watched her laugh and then glared at me, officially guaranteeing me a lousy grade if I ever found myself in his class.

Ms. Ferrell chuckled, too, which made me feel good as usual—I loved making her laugh, because even though I associated her with homework, books, and reading, I actually liked her a lot as a person.

"I'm looking forward to Tuesday," she said, and for a second I had no idea what she was talking about.

And then I remembered. Oh, yeah.

I was presenting my Position Paper on Tuesday.

As in, six days from now.

"I'm looking forward to it, too," I said.

Ms. Axlerod laughed again, even though this time I wasn't trying to be funny at all.

Sunday night—two days before I had to present my Position Paper—I suddenly felt kind of guilty.

It wasn't Jake reading the books for me that made me feel guilty.

And it wasn't my parents and my sister not knowing that he was reading the books for me that made me feel guilty.

It was that Jake was over for dinner, and my parents were telling him that he was such a good influence on me and how proud they were that I was reading so much and working so hard on my Position Paper. And that Jake had sneaked a glance at me and kind of shrugged as if to say, *If they only knew.*

It was the combination of all those things that made me feel guilty.

I had told my parents about a week before that I was writing about cliques in middle school, and they had agreed that it was a great topic to explore. I had showed them the books I was using for my research, which they thought looked fascinating.

Then I had promptly given the books to Jake the next day in school.

Now, all of a sudden at dinner, I was having pangs of guilt.

Feelings can be so inconvenient.

To clear my conscience, I decided to clear the dishes.

"Can I get you boys any dessert before you go off to study?" my mom asked.

"No, thanks," I said, just as Jake said, "Yes, please." I wanted to get out of there as quickly as possible. Jake wanted ice cream.

He was digging into some mint chocolate chip when the conversation got even more awkward.

"So Charlie Joe tells us you're dating Hannah Spivero," my dad said.

"When did I say that?" I complained. I had no idea where he got his information. How is it that parents always seem to know stuff?

Megan tried to help. "Dad," she said, "middle-school boys don't like to talk about things like that."

But Jake was one middle-school boy who was perfectly happy to talk about things like that, particularly when the things in question had to do with his new girlfriend.

"Yeah, it's going really well. I can't believe it," Jake said. "And it's all thanks to Charlie Joe."

I froze. Jake immediately looked at me, like, *oops*.

My parents, thank God, sat there kind of clueless. Megan said to me, "You're the one who set them up? Why would you do that? I thought *you* were like totally in love with Hannah Spivero."

"Not anymore," I said, and then by way of changing the

subject, I said to Jake, "So you like mint chocolate chip, huh? I'm a coffee man myself."

Upstairs in my room, Jake gave me incredibly helpful, brilliantly written, chapter-by-chapter synopses of each book I was supposed to read.

It probably took him about a half an hour to write them.

"These were actually really cool books," he said. "You picked a really interesting topic."

"Thanks," I said. "Really, thanks for everything, dude. You totally saved my life!"

Jake sat down on my bed.

"Why do you hate reading so much?"

I had guilt on the brain, three synopses to read and no time for chitchat, so I just said, "I don't know, I just do."

He just shook his head sadly. "You don't know what you're missing."

Charlie Joe's Tip #21

THERE ARE THINGS YOU NEED TO MAKE SURE YOU KNOW WHEN TELLING SOMEONE YOU DID READ A BOOK, WHEN YOU ACTUALLY DIDN'T READ THE BOOK:

1) *The title*
2) *The author*
3) *What's on the cover*
4) *How long it is (approximate)*
5) *The name of the main character*
6) *The name of anyone who dies*
7) *The names of any animals*
8) *How long it took to read*
9) *What happened in a specific chapter*
10) *If you liked it or not*

Tuesday morning, 11:10 a.m.

You know that drop of sweat that suddenly appears on your forehead when you get nervous?

And then it slowly trickles down your cheek, like a tear your brain sheds because it's so sad that you got yourself into this situation?

Well, that drop of sweat was about halfway through its journey when I got up in front of the class to deliver my Position Paper.

Ms. Ferrell was there, of course. But since this was the big academic event of the year, so was the rest of the English department: Mr. Simms, Ms. Cohen, and Dr. Jamison, who was obviously the most important person in the school because he was the only doctor (although I personally never saw him heal anyone).

What seemed like the entire free world was also there, even though it was only the twenty-two other kids in my English class.

I cleared my throat. If only I could have cleared the room.

"Hi everyone, my name is Charlie Joe Jackson," I began in a scholarly fashion. I saw Timmy roll his eyes. "Thank you for coming today."

What choice did they have?

"My Position Paper is entitled 'From Friends to Rivals: How the Pressures Facing Kids Today Makes Them Form Cliques, or Teams, to Face Off Against One Another.'"

Hold your applause.

I plowed ahead. "The books I read for this project are as follows: *The Clique as Crutch*, by Marvin S. Hackett; *Too Many Clubs, Too Little Time*, by Sheila Warburg; and *The Modern Superkid*, by Frederick and Catherine Wilson."

I took a quick glance at the teachers to see if anyone seemed like they'd heard of the books—hoping they hadn't, of course—but I couldn't tell, so I continued.

This was my awesome first sentence:

Hi everyone, my name is Charlie Joe Jackson

"It is my contention that because kids in today's society are under so much pressure to excel, and they spend so much time in studies and extracurricular activities, that they don't develop the necessary social skills to interact with all their peers, and therefore only socialize with those with their immediate interests, leading to cliques, clubs, and other forms of separation that are ultimately detrimental to the developmental and maturation process as kids try to become adults."

Too run-on?

* * *

I presented my paper with a minimum of slip-ups, making some good points along the way. I mean, if you want to be technical about it, I'm sure I repeated the same points a few times—who doesn't? But at the same time, I felt fairly confident that I was doing a pretty good job.

In any event, I had some special surprises planned for the end of my presentation. I was saving the best for last.

"Up to this point," I announced, "I have given a fairly traditional Position Paper. I read the books, did the research, wrote a thesis statement, and backed up my thesis with facts and figures." I took a deep breath. Here goes. "But now, ladies and gentlemen, I would like to offer you specific evidence of how kids can fight back, and worry less about getting straight A's and getting into high school honors classes, and concentrate more on getting to know all the cool and different kinds of kids around them. Because it can be done. And the most important thing is the kids themselves want it to happen."

I nodded to Timmy, and he stood up. "My name is Timmy McGibney. I usually hang around with kids who like to skateboard and snowboard, but yesterday I had a long conversation with Casey who's in the orchestra, and he was really nice."

I nodded to Pete Milano, who got up, smirking. "I think about sports like all day every day, but one time my parents

took me to see a Broadway musical, and it was pretty good."
He sat down amidst snickering from his fellow jocks.

I nodded to Eliza, and she got up. "A lot of kids consider me the most beautiful girl in the grade, but that doesn't mean I only want to hang out with other beautiful girls." Okay, she didn't totally stick to script, but moving on . . .

Katie popped up out of her chair. "For a while I was a dork, then I was a goth, then I was a skater, then I was a loser, then I was a winner, then I finally discovered who I really was: just a girl." She grinned at me and sat down.

Let's just say it, Katie Friedman is plain awesome.

I snuck another glance at the teachers, who were clearly enjoying the show-and-tell. It was going well so far.

Time for the big finish.

* * *

I put my paper down on Ms. Ferrell's desk as if I were done.

"Thank you all for listening," I said, wrapping up. "I hope we've all learned an important lesson here today. Let kids be kids, and guess what? They just might surprise you."

I headed to my seat to some healthy applause. I was pretty sure it was B+ applause at least. And then, right on cue . . .

"Wait a second."

Everyone stopped clapping . . . stopped talking . . . stopped everything.

Hannah Spivero had stood up.

Not just on the floor.

Not just on her chair.

Yup, Hannah Spivero—the girl of my dreams—was standing on her *desk*.

"I have something to say," she announced grandly. She waited a beat for the suspense to build—she was a natural performer, it turned out—before going on.

"I guess by now everyone knows that Jake and I are going out."

We did.

"When Jake first asked me out, I thought he was crazy," Hannah continued. "Why would I ever go out with someone like Jake? All my friends laughed." She looked at Jake,

who looked back, self-consciously. "But I decided, so what? Who was I to judge him just because he wore glasses and played violin and was in the chess club? Maybe I should give him a chance."

She paused, milking the moment. "It turned out to be the best decision I ever made."

Oh man, was she good.

Then Hannah got down off her desk. She walked to the front of the room, then slowly, almost ceremoniously, turned around and walked straight up to Jake Katz.

"I really like you," said my never-to-be girlfriend to her boyfriend, right before leaning over and giving him a kiss on his glowing, blushing, bright red cheek.

✳ ✳ ✳

The place erupted. Chaos. Pandemonium. Anarchy. Bedlam. (Thesaurus.com—check it out.)

Jake nearly had a heart attack. (And if he had, he would have died a happy man.)

And right at my moment of triumph, I realized something about myself. When I came up with the plan to set up Jake and Hannah, I told myself they wouldn't actually fall for each other, yet somehow I knew it would happen. But it didn't matter.

That's how desperate I was to avoid reading. I was willing to see the girl of my dreams kiss someone else.

It was both the greatest and worst moment of my life.

Apparently, I wasn't quite finished.

Ms. Ferrell shushed the crowd, which took some doing.

"A very impressive presentation, Charlie Joe," she said, stating the obvious. "And extremely theatrical. But as you know, the teachers often like to ask some follow-up questions, just to ensure that you have complete command of the material."

Are you kidding? Complete command of the material? Did you or did you not just see me rock this room?

"Of course," I said.

Dr. Jamison went first. "Mr. Jackson, first of all, I want to tell you how much I enjoyed your paper, and I admire the topic you chose. But I am curious, which of the books did you find most helped you in your research?"

Talk about a softball! The good doctor had lobbed one over the plate. I could smack this one out of the park, thanks to Charlie Joe's Tip #21.

"I'm glad you asked that, Dr. Jamison. I really enjoyed all the books I read, but if I were forced to pick my most valuable resource, it would have to be *Modern Superkid*, by Frederick and Catherine Wilson. From the image of the four-headed child on the cover, to the fascinating example of the overworked violin prodigy in chapter seven, I found the book to be extremely compelling. I guess the best way to describe how interesting I found this book was that it was 278 pages long, and yet it went by in a flash."

The teachers all nodded, and I thought I was home free, until Mr. Simms said, "I remember that book."

Huh.

Just keep nodding, I told myself.

"And I concur," he continued, "the violin prodigy story is an invaluable cautionary tale for all parents who are thinking of overloading their children with a myriad of activities."

I kind of knew what *concur* meant, and I had no idea what *myriad* meant, but I knew what all the other words meant, and they were put together in an order that made me very happy. So I nodded in agreement, and Mr. Simms smiled.

Ms. Cohen was up next. "Charlie Joe, I'm not completely convinced that all the blame can be placed at the feet of adults. The children are willing participants in this whole vicious cycle. Can you please explain how the various books you've read illuminated your theories on adult pressure versus peer pressure? Are they clear in delineating the differences between the two?"

Stay calm, my young friend, stay calm . . . form a quick mental image of Jake's synopses in your mind . . . ah, here they are . . . and . . . Go!

"Well, Ms. Cohen, that's a very good question. All the books did stress how the kids are ultimately responsible for changing their own behavior, but perhaps it is best explained by Sheila Warburg, in her book *Too Many Clubs, Too Little Time*. She says in Chapter 3, which is entitled 'Taking Back Your Lives,' that every kid ultimately has to make their own decisions, that they can't assume that just because their parents are adults, that ultimately every decision they make is ultimately the correct one."

I was vaguely aware that I'd used the word *ultimately* four times in that explanation, but I didn't care. You do what you have to do.

Ms. Ferrell stood up, which was the equivalent of a Get Out of Jail Free card.

"Well, Charlie Joe, I have to say you handled yourself extremely well. I'm very proud of you. Good job."

I nodded and sat down. Everyone clapped again. The sweat on my forehead was just starting to dry. I started to get some feeling back in my tongue.

So this is what freedom tasted like.

Show of hands: who wants a short chapter?
It's unanimous.

Katie cornered me immediately after class.

"You were amazing in there," she said. For some strange reason, it was right at that moment that I realized she had fewer freckles than she used to.

When did that happen?

"Thanks," I said.

We looked at each other for a few seconds too long, and suddenly it got a little weird.

Katie and I have always had a mutual understanding that we're better off as friends. We were better as friends in first grade, and we'll be better off as friends when we're eighty years old.

In other words, it would never work between us.

Or would it?

"Come on," she said. "You can't be serious."

Like always, she knew exactly what I was thinking.

I hated and loved that about her.

"What?"

"You know what." She pulled me away from the kids who were still slapping me on the back after my triumph. "It would never work, you and me. We care about each other way too much."

That may have been the smartest thing anyone ever said to me.

I hugged her. "You're the best girlfriend I ever had."

She hugged me back. "By girlfriend you mean girl-slash-friend, right?"

"Of course," I said, although I wasn't entirely sure.

✳ ✳ ✳

I found Jake—the man of the hour—all alone in the boys' room, cleaning his glasses.

"That was so awesome," I said, clapping him on the back. "Thanks again. You are so the man."

He didn't look up.

"Do you think she might actually like me?" he asked worriedly. "I mean, now that it's over, and you did the

168

paper . . . do you think she'll still want to go out with me?"

He blinked, as if he'd just woken up from a dream—a dream called Hannah Spivero.

"I think so," I answered, and I realized as I said it that I actually meant it. "Believe it or not, I really think so, dude."

"I THINK SO, TOO!" Jake yelled, and he let out a loud WHOOP! and started jumping up and down and pounding on the paper towel dispenser.

"She likes me! She likes me! Yo everyone, Hannah Spivero likes ME!" he shouted over and over again to the world, even though we were the only people there.

As I watched him the first thing I thought was, this kid is crazy.

The second thing I thought was, I'd be reacting the same exact way.

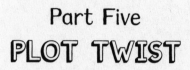

Part Five
PLOT TWIST

Charlie Joe's Tip #22

ALWAYS BE WARY OF THE PLOT TWIST.

Books with a last-second plot twist are just desperately trying to hold your attention until the last minute.

Which is a shame, since the author could have saved us all a lot of trouble by just ending the book earlier.

I've noticed that this book has changed a lot since I started it.

It's become more like a book book.

Which is not the book I set out to write.

I'm not sure what happened.

No one liked to admit it, but everyone looked forward to the last big social event of the school year.

The name, The Year-End Dance, was boring and nerdy. But the ingredients—pizza, an ice-cream sundae bar, and dancing close to girls—were all right on the money.

It was the last weekend of the year. There were only two days left of school, that last random Monday and Tuesday that never make any sense, because all the tests and homework are done, and nobody does anything but walk around saying good-bye, signing yearbooks, and giving each other hugs. (The whole hugging thing has gotten pretty out of control, by the way. Now kids hug if they haven't seen each other for three whole minutes. They should drop Sex Education and replace it with Hug Education.)

And people were starting to talk about their summer plans.

I was traditionally a proud summer slacker, but this was the year my parents had decided I would do something productive, like go to soccer camp, or get a babysitting job, or—it makes my skin twitch just writing this—take a summer school class.

But that was before my Position Paper triumph. The pleasure my parents took in my achievement (they had finally read my Paper, and loved it) made me think I might be able to avoid any additional academic duty over the summer; and when I mentioned that I needed a new bathing suit, my mom didn't give me her usual "you can go to the beach on weekends, after you do your chores and read at least one complete book during the week" speech.

Maybe they were proud of me, maybe they had just given up, or maybe it was a combination of both—but it was starting to look like the summer was shaping up to be chock full of my favorite activity.

Nada.

✳✳✳

Anyway, on the day of the dance, the whole school was buzzing with anticipation, and the usual last-minute rush of boys asking girls to go was happening at a record-setting pace. As for myself, ever since the day four months ago when Eliza thought I was asking her, I had wondered who I would end up going with. I considered asking about thirty girls.

I ended up asking Timmy McGibney and Pete Milano.

✳✳✳

I got to the dance right on time—forty-five minutes late.

It was dark, it was sweaty, it was impossible to hear anyone talk.

In other words, it was just right.

Timmy, Pete, and I were hanging out, trying to decide if we should a) ask specific girls to dance, b) join the general clump of dancers, or c) shoot baskets for a few minutes in the gym while deciding how to approach the whole dancing situation.

Pete had a firm opinion. "Dudes, you don't ask a girl to dance at these kinds of things. That totally pins you down. You just dive into the pile, and dance with all of 'em at once! Right, C.J.?" he said to me, punching my arm. Pete was a puncher.

"Right," I said, scanning the crowd for a couple of faces that I hadn't yet seen. It took me a minute to find Katie, who was hanging out with her usual friends, doing her usual thing (texting them).

I caught her eye and waved, and she smiled and waved back. I know, not exactly a momentous event, but it made me feel good, so I thought I'd tell you about it.

Mainly because it was just about the last thing that made me feel good that night. Or ever.

Another punch on the arm from Pete. "Whoa!" he said, pointing at the front door.

I looked. Whoa indeed.

Coming through the door was Hannah Spivero, and holding her hand was a kid who used to be Jake Katz.

***

You know that thing in cartoons where a character sees something he doesn't believe, so he rubs his eyes, shakes his head, and looks again?

Well, I'm pretty sure that's what I did.

Jake bore only a passing resemblance to his former self. He wasn't wearing his glasses—so either he couldn't see or he was finally wearing those contact lenses his parents were begging him to get. His clothes were all new and actually fit, and he moussed up his hair to the point where it would have made a porcupine jealous.

He looked good.

Hannah, on the other hand, looked like she always looked. Perfect.

Everybody turned to stare as the happy couple entered the cafeteria. Trailing behind them and basking in their reflected glory was Teddy Spivero, Hannah's shallow-end-of-the-gene-pool twin brother.

Teddy surveyed the crowd until he found what he was looking for.

Me.

"Yo, Jerko Jackson," he bellowed, using a beloved nickname I hadn't heard since fourth grade. He pointed at Jake and his sister. "Check it out—still going strong!"

Timmy nudged my shoulder—he was a nudger—and turned to me with a jealous look on his face.

"Are they still going out?" He wasn't so much asking me as asking the universe how a thing like this could happen.

I could feel the universe shrug in response.

"It would appear so," I said testily. I was a little annoyed at him. What right did he have to be jealous? He'd dated her for about seven hours, whereas I'd loved her for about seven years.

Teddy bounded over to us like a St. Bernard who'd had too much caffeine. "PEOPLES!"

Did Teddy Spivero just say "peoples"?

He elbowed me right in the stomach. (He was an elbower.) "I bet you thought it wouldn't last more than a minute, huh? Well look at the two of 'em now, gettin' ready to hit the dance floor and do a little bit of the old ookie ookie."

"Ookie ookie?" "Peoples?" Say what you will about Teddy Spivero—which is that he is an idiot—he had apparently come up with his own language, and I had to admit it had a certain style.

"I couldn't be more happy for them," I said, trying to sound happy for them.

Jake brought Hannah over supposedly to say hello, but really to take a sort of victory lap. "Hey, Charlie Joe," he said, while trying to drape his arm around Hannah's shoulders but only reaching the middle of her back. "How's it going? Hey, Timmy. Hey, Pete."

We all mumbled something that sounded kind of like "Hey, Jake."

Jake looked at me. "You were right. People from very different cliques can thrive together if only given the chance."

Hannah looked at me. "You are so smart sometimes, Charlie Joe Jackson."

"It's nice to be smart," I said, dumbly.

Remember back in chapter forty-six when Jake was happy with the idea of going to the dance solo, because if he went with a girl he would have felt tied down, and wouldn't have been able to go get a drink or hang out with his friends whenever he wanted?

Yeah, well, it turns out he didn't end up talking to his friends barely at all, and he didn't make it to the punch bowl very often.

And you know what?

He didn't seem all that devastated about it.

Pete's idea, dancing with everybody in a big clump, turned out to be totally fun. We spent most of the night jumping up and down with pretty much the entire grade, just a bunch of kids together, boys and girls, having a blast, putting the stress and pressure of another school year behind us.

At one point during the heat of the moment, I actually had a weird feeling that I was going to miss school.

That was pretty creepy.

Then came the song where the girls are supposed to ask the boys to dance. Everyone was pairing off, and I saw Eliza heading over to me. It occurred to me that there were worse things in the world than dancing with the prettiest girl in school.

"Hey, Charlie Joe."

"Hey, Lize."

She flipped her hair a few times. "I just wanted you to know that even though you never ended up asking me to the dance, I'm not mad. But even so, I won't be asking you to dance, because you can lead a horse to water, but you can't make him eat."

I looked at her. "I think it's 'you can't make him drink.' You know, since it's water?"

She squinted, considering the possibility.

"Whatever," she said, and she meant it.

$$* * *$$

As Eliza departed, Katie arrived.

"What was that about?"

"Oh, you know, the usual," I said. "She likes me, I don't like her, but somehow I'm the one who ends up standing there alone like a doofus."

"Well, does the doofus want to dance?" Katie always knew just what to say.

I looked at her gratefully. "I thought you'd never ask."

It was one of those Coldplay songs that's neither fast nor slow, so we just kind of looked at each other and shuffled back and forth.

"Did you have a good year?" she asked. She didn't mess around; she always went straight for the big questions that were far too complicated for someone like me to answer.

"Pretty good," I said. I was watching Jake and Hannah dance. They were in their own little world, and no one else was invited.

"'Pretty good?'" she echoed. "What does that mean? Did you grow? Did you learn anything? Or are you still the same Charlie Joe Jackson that I usually find adorable but sometimes find impossible?"

"What?" I answered, distractedly.

She saw me staring at Jake and Hannah, rolled her eyes, and sighed.

"This whole thing was your idea, don't forget," she said, as if I could ever forget.

"I know. And it worked like a charm," I said glumly. "I'm a genius."

"Be happy for them," she said in her wise, I'm-going-to-be-a-therapist-someday voice. "You can be shocked, you can be confused, and you can be a little freaked out. But try to be just a little bit happy for them. Can you do that?"

I looked at her, and thought for a second.

"Want to get some punch?"

A couple of sweaty hours later, Phil
Manning and Celia Barbarossa came in second in the vot-
ing for king and queen of the dance. I was really happy for
them. They were a perfectly normal couple except for the
fact that they'd been going out since fourth grade, were
completely devoted to each other, and everyone was pretty
sure they'd get married and live happily ever after.

Guess which couple came in first?

I'll give you a hint: one's a Goddess and one's taking
ninth-grade algebra.

I was somewhat less happy for them.

In our school, the two top couples get to make a little
speech. It was a year-end-dance tradition.

Did I ever mention I officially hate traditions?

Phil and Celia gave a lovely speech, all about the sanc-
tity of their love (whatever that means), thereby proving
beyond a shadow of a doubt that they were way too emo-
tionally mature for the rest of us.

Then it was Hannah and Jake's turn. Hannah took the
microphone first, caressing it like she was an American
Idol finalist, about to do a deeply emotional interpretation
of Aerosmith's "Walk This Way."

"Jake and I stand here before you as an example of how opposites attract, and how you can never predict who will end up liking whom," she purred, making googly eyes at her dork-turned-dreamboat. "Like The Beatles once said, 'the love you make is equal to the love you take,'" she added, probably unaware that she was reminding me I had given up not one but two things: any shot at her love and my most precious material possession.

She handed the mike to Jake, and bent down (she was three inches taller than him) to give him a kiss on the cheek.

Timmy and I both touched our own cheeks involuntarily.

"My name is Jake Katz," Jake said, in that way that made you realize he was going to go on for a while. "I have never had a girlfriend. I do really well in school but I'm not really that popular or anything."

I suddenly got a weird feeling in my stomach. Jake was being honest. Very honest.

Too honest.

"I tried to convince myself that I was perfectly happy. I told myself I would be a famous writer someday, and when I was rich and successful I'd have all the girls in the world, and everything would be fantastic." He reached up to adjust his glasses, momentarily forgetting that he wasn't wearing them. "But really I was just kind of fooling myself, because actually I was pretty lonely."

Uh-oh. I could tell he was being emotional and not thinking.

"So when Charlie Joe Jackson told me about his idea to fix me up with Hannah, I didn't get it," he said next.

One cat, officially out of the bag.

All eyes turned to me.

My eyes turned to the fire exits, in case I would need one.

Jake continued. "He's my friend, but I couldn't help but think that maybe it was some kind of cruel joke. You know, kind of like that movie *Carrie*."

Wow, interesting example there, dude. Have you ever seen *Carrie?* The unbelievably scary movie where the loser girl with supernatural powers is picked on by all the kids in her grade, and is set up with the popular boy as a practical joke, until she gets her revenge by burning them all to death at the YEAR-END DANCE?

Suddenly, *everybody* was looking for the fire exits.

Jake looked at Hannah and for one brief wonderful moment I thought maybe he wouldn't have the nerve to continue.

Then she smiled at him, and off he went.

"But then, when Charlie Joe explained about his Position Paper, and how he wanted to prove that cliques were wrong and could be overcome, I was glad to be part of his noble experiment. And I wanted to find out if the most popular girl and the dorkiest kid in the grade could find true happiness together, too."

Then Jake looked directly at me, and suddenly, for some strange reason, I knew exactly what was about to happen. I knew that I would be powerless to stop it, that I would just have to let it happen. No fire exits. No hole in the ground to crawl into. No nothing.

"But it wasn't until Charlie Joe asked me to read his books for the Position Paper for him," Jake said, sealing my fate, "that I realized just how deeply entrenched cliques were in our society."

It seemed like the room went dead silent right then. Except for the sound of my heart pounding, of course, which was deafening.

"Every school has them, and it seems like every school is powerless to stop them," Jake said, getting more passionate by the second. "So if somehow I could be just a small part in ending the cliques in our small corner of the world, then I would have done something really, really, cool."

Then Jake took his girlfriend's hand. And even though I knew my life as I knew it was about to end, I couldn't help but be a little bit touched.

"So we started going out," Jake said, raising his voice to be heard over the increasing din. "And three days ago, Hannah Spivero kissed me in front of the whole world."

Jake raised his arms to heavens, as if to say thank you.

"Hannah Spivero!"

A lot of kids missed his second "Hannah Spivero!"—which was as pure a declaration of love as you'll ever hear —because the room had exploded in a lollaplooza of sound. And everywhere I looked, kids were pointing at me and laughing.

You are so screwed!

Pete Milano elbowed me in the ribs. "You are so screwed!" he said, helpfully.

I felt like I was having one of those out-of-body experiences, which sounds kind of cool, but in this case most definitely was not.

I looked around, hoping for a friendly face, and I caught a quick glimpse of Katie and Ms. Ferrell. Their faces didn't look friendly. They looked crushed.

That made me feel bad.

Then I saw Mr. Radonski heading over to my table.

That made me feel worse.

Meanwhile, Jake was still up on the stage, confused. Of course, he had no idea what he had just said. He had no idea that he had just ruined my life. It wasn't his fault. He was in love. He was caught up in the moment.

I was just caught, period.

***

When Jake uttered the fateful words, "But it wasn't
until Charlie Joe asked me to read his books for the Position Paper for him," the only one in the whole building
who wasn't surprised was Timmy.

Timmy, who had been my co-conspirator for years.
Timmy, the only one who knew what I was up to—the
one, in fact, who had helped me refine the plan when it
was just a dream in my head—nudged me one last time,
just as Mr. Radonski reached for my arm.

"Dude, you probably should have just read the books,"
he said.

***

The second-to-last thing I remember from that
night was catching Katie's eye as I left the dance. She was
waving good-bye, sadly, as if she wasn't going to see me
again for a long time. Which was pretty much true.

And the very last thing I remember was Mr. Radonski
escorting me out of the cafeteria just as the music kicked
back in: "I Wanna Rock and Roll All Night," by Kiss.

"Dang it, I love this song," said Mr. Radonski as we
headed out—as if he needed another reason to hate me.

Part Six
ALMOST HOME

61

I've been grounded before, and I'll be grounded again.

This time, I would probably be grounded for six years, but as we all know, the good thing about being grounded is that it never really lasts that long.

I mean, you can get grounded for longer and longer periods of time, you can even get grounded for life, but when you think about it, the average grounding really only lasts approximately 5.5 days, because by then everybody is pretty much sick of you hanging around the house whining all the time.

I was already planning on being as whiny as possible.

* * *

I was waiting in the gym for my parents to pick me up from the dance when Mr. Radonski showed me his tattoo.

"See this?" he said, rolling back his right shirtsleeve to reveal a large bald

eagle smoking a cigar. "I got this baby in the service. Took me six hours. Getting that tattoo was by far the most painful thing I've ever had to endure in my life."

He leaned in close, close enough for me to recognize the brand of tomato sauce he'd had for dinner.

"But that pain is going to feel like walking on a bed of marshmallows compared to the hell I'm going to put you through in my class next year."

I love you, too, Mr. Radonski.

I was trying to figure out how to convince my parents to move to another state, when lo and behold, they walked through the door.

My dad is one of those guys who never loses his temper, but when he does, look out. And every great once in a while, he gets so mad that you feel it even before he says a word.

This was one of those times.

I could tell he was trying not to blow when he came through the door. His eyes were very narrow and his body was kind of hunched over, and I could tell that what he felt most—more than anger, or disappointment, or frustration—was shame.

"Hi, I'm James Jackson," he said to Mr. Radonski, and they shook hands. "I want to thank you for looking after my son, and I apologize for whatever trouble he's caused you tonight."

"No problem," Mr. Radonski said, giving no indication that he'd put the fear of God in me about thirty-eight seconds earlier.

"Hi, Bill," my mom said as she walked through the door. She knew Mr. Radonski because she had subbed at our school a few times over the years.

She smiled warmly at him, which was pretty impressive considering there was a tear in her eye.

"Nice to see you again, Claire," Mr. Radonski said, also smiling, like he was about to tell her that I was the greatest kid in the world.

My dad sat down next to me and just looked at me for what felt like ten years. Then he slowly shook his head.

"Let's go home," he said.

And we went home.

At first, I felt terrible.

That night, as expected, I was grounded indefinitely. Which was fine by me, because there wasn't anybody I particularly wanted to see.

I had to give up my cell phone, which was also fine by me, because there wasn't anybody I particularly wanted to text or talk to.

I had to give up my computer, which was fine by me, because . . . well, you get the idea.

I spent that entire weekend in my room, staring at the walls, looking back on everything that had happened, trying to figure out if I was a horrible person.

Eventually I came to the conclusion that I wasn't a completely horrible person, and I felt a lot better.

I was definitely a careless person. Possibly a lazy person, although as we all know, it takes a lot of work to avoid reading. And maybe I was a slightly scheming person. But horrible? Come on. Remember, I knew horrible. I knew Teddy Spivero.

And yeah, I did some dumb things. I put Jake Katz in a bad position where he did something he wasn't supposed to do, and it was quite possible he would get in a little trouble, but that's a small price to pay for Hannah Spivero looking you in the eyes and saying "I really, really like you."

And yeah, Jake read all the books for me, but I memorized his notes, and wrote the whole presentation, and had the idea for the grande finale with all the drama and announcements and stuff. Come on, that was pretty original, you gotta admit.

Don't get me wrong, I still felt bad, but I was done beating myself up. What good would it do? And it's not like I'm the only kid in all of recorded history who ever tried to get away with something.

In fact, if I'm not mistaken, it's exactly that kind of good old-fashioned creativity that's made America the great nation it is today.

Suddenly, I wanted my cell phone back. And my computer. And my video games.

But I wouldn't see any of them again until I went back to school.

Next year.

By Sunday night, I felt a different kind of terrible.

I'd moved on from the I'm-a-horrible-person kind of terrible to the man-this-summer-is-going-to-stink kind of terrible.

Monday was yearbook-signing day
for the entire student body, minus one.

Guess who was the one?

I guess now's as good a time as any to introduce you to Mrs. Sleep, the principal of our school.

I kid you not, that is her name.

You know that saying that helps you tell the difference between princiPAL and princiPLE? "The principal is your pal?"

Well, whoever invented that saying never met Mrs. Sleep.

It's not that she was a mean, awful person. It's just that she was really old-fashioned.

She was so old-fashioned that even the *teachers* called her Mrs. Sleep. She was so old-fashioned that her first name, which nobody ever used, was Enid.

She was tall, and smelled a little dusty, and looked kind of like Eleanor Roosevelt on a bad hair day.

But most important, she had a huge scary chair behind a huge scary desk in a huge scary office, and right at that moment she was sitting in that very chair staring down at me.

I was as prepared as I could be. I knew Timmy and Katie had been to the principal's office earlier that day, and I figured they were kind of like the appetizers.

I was the main course.

And the main course was sitting in the chair on the other side of Mrs. Sleep's desk, ready to be devoured.

It felt like I was squeezed into one of my sister's dollhouse chairs she used to play with, back when she was into dollhouses.

Ms. Ferrell was there, too. She did the talking, while Mrs. Sleep just stared down at me like a disapproving owl.

I knew how disappointed Ms. Ferrell was in me, so I couldn't really look her in the eye.

She cleared her throat nervously. Why was she nervous? It was my funeral, not hers.

"I want you to know that your friends are very loyal to you," Ms. Ferrell began, "and they shared the following information with Mrs. Sleep and myself very reluctantly."

That was nice to know. I was sure that at some point in the very, very distant future, I would learn to appreciate it.

"According to Timothy McGibney, you and he have had an arrangement for several years, in which you buy him snacks in the cafeteria and he reads your assigned books, in order to tell you what's in them."

She waited for a response. I had none, so she continued.

"And according to Katherine Friedman, you were famous for reading as little as possible. In fact, you were quite proud of it, and carried it around as a sort of badge of honor."

Ouch. That one left a mark.

For a split second, I couldn't believe I'd been betrayed by my friends.

But in the next second, I realized I couldn't really blame Timmy or Katie for spilling the beans.

After all, they had been sitting in the same chair that I was sitting in right now.

And short of reading the collected works of Mark Twain, I can't think of a scarier situation.

Looking at some sort of report, Mrs. Sleep asked Ms. Ferrell, "And what of Jacob Katz? Has he confirmed what he said at the dance, that he read Mr. Jackson's books for the Position Paper, in exchange for a date with Hannah Spivero?" That wasn't technically true, it wasn't that he HAD to read the books in order to go out with Hannah, it just seemed that way now. But it was too late, the damage was done.

Mrs. Sleep was looking at me like I was a kitten killer. Or worse.

And then Ms. Ferrell did a strange thing. First she paused. Then she said, "In fact, Jacob Katz has retracted what he said, and is now denying that Charlie Joe Jackson ever asked him to do any such thing. In fact, Jacob said the whole thing was his idea."

Wait, WHAT?!

At that very moment, I officially decided that Jake Katz—book-reader, miracle-baseball-catch-maker, contact-lens-wearer, hair-mousser—was 100 percent worthy of Hannah's love.

＊＊＊

Mrs. Sleep looked at me over her reading glasses. "Well, Charles Joseph? Is Mr. Katz telling the truth, or is he protecting you? Do you care to enlighten us?"

I took probably the deepest breath of my life.

Then I did something that goes against every bone of my body, every fiber of my being, every ounce of my personality, and against everything that has made me the remarkable person I am today.

I told the truth.

Charlie Joe's Tip #23

IT'S POSSIBLE TO DISLIKE READING AND STILL BE GOOD AT WRITING.

Just because I don't like to read doesn't mean I can't write.

In fact, I'm a pretty solid writer. For example, I'm very good at similes, metaphors, and oxymorons.

Here's an example of a simile:

Finding out I had to read that book was as disappointing as a rainy summer day.

Here's an example of a metaphor:

I slogged my way through that book in about a year.

And here are some helpful oxymorons:

1. *good book*
2. *happy reader*
3. *important author*
4. *nice library*
5. *favorite bookstore*

Did I mention that my parents were in the principal's office, too?

They weren't in very good moods.

My dad had taken the day off from work, which I thought might have made him happy, but for some reason didn't, and my mom had missed yoga, which threw off her "center of being," and therefore made her grumpy.

In any event, they were sitting in these weird little aluminum folding chairs that looked like they were left over from the time Mrs. Sleep was a student at the school.

Though I had bigger things on my mind, I did take a minute to notice how ridiculous my parents looked in those chairs.

After I told everyone that Jake was just covering for me and that I had, in fact, asked Jake Katz to read the books for me, and after I insisted that it was all my fault, and after I begged that Jake not be punished, which they said they would "look into"—after all that, they sent me to the outer office while they discussed my punishment.

It was kind of like being strapped into the electric chair, then suddenly being sent to wait outside while they fixed one of the switches.

I waited there for ten minutes, while several kids came in so the school secretary could sign their yearbooks. When they saw me, they acted like they felt sorry for me, until they giggled.

Suddenly Ms. Ferrell poked her head out of Mrs. Sleep's office.

"Would you come back in here please, Mr. Jackson?"

Mr. Jackson? I got up with a heavy sigh and headed in behind her.

"You're going to love this, Charlie Joe," she said, chuckling.

I was pretty sure she was being sarcastic.

✳ ✳ ✳

I took my seat. Everyone was silent, waiting for Mrs. Sleep to speak. This was her moment. This was what she lived for.

"Charles Joseph Jackson, I do hope you realize the pain you've caused not only your fellow students, but also the teachers who are trying to guide you, and your parents, who love you so much," she began.

I didn't buy the student-pain thing—everybody seemed to be having a pretty darn good time running around getting ready for the summer and feeling relieved they weren't me—but I did feel bad about letting down Ms. Ferrell, and really bad about embarrassing my parents. (So far, they hadn't found out that Megan had read a book for me, too. Thank God for small favors.)

Mrs. Sleep came around and sat on the front of her desk. She did this when she was getting ready to break out the big guns. "There are several courses of action we could take here. Obviously suspension is not an option, because the school year is essentially over."

For some reason that didn't make me feel better.

"And your parents have told me of all the many times they've tried to get you to read on your own, with absolutely no success."

No argument from me.

I was hoping she was going to tell me to write "I will never not read my assigned book again" over and over again on the blackboard like Bart Simpson, but I was pretty sure that's not what she had in mind.

The principal peered down at me in that time-honored, principally way. "Apart from finding a suitable punishment for your recent infraction, it is clear that you need to learn how vital reading is to your growth and development, both as a student and as a young person."

Mrs. Sleep pushed her glasses back up the bridge of her nose, which magnified her eyes into huge flying saucers.

"So, after consulting with both Ms. Ferrell and your parents, we have decided on a course of action for you that we feel is reasonable and appropriate."

I liked the sound of *reasonable*. I didn't like the sound of *appropriate*.

Mrs. Sleep nodded to Ms. Ferrell, who talked next. "Charlie Joe, I've had you in my class for a year now, and I know how bright you are. Despite your best efforts to deny yourself knowledge, you have learned quite a bit in school, and you are an imaginative, creative thinker. Perhaps even more creative than we realized, in ways that may not always reflect the best judgment on your part. And we'd like to help you channel that creativity in a more constructive way."

Why did this feel like the calm before the storm?

"So we are going to give you a choice."

I looked at my parents, who were both nodding at Ms. Ferrell.

They were in on it.

"The first option," Ms. Ferrell continued, "is to read ten books over the course of the summer, and write a five-page book report on each one."

I think I threw up a little in my mouth. Somehow I managed to sputter, "Ten books?!" in disbelief. "What's the other choice?"

It seemed like they were all dying to answer, but Mrs. Sleep got there first.

"The other option is to *write* a book. A book no less than 150 pages in length, on any topic you choose."

It felt like time stopped as they waited for me to object. Which I did, even though by that point I could barely talk.

"You're kidding, right?" I wheeezed.

Mrs. Sleep was more than happy to answer, her eyes looking scarier than ever behind those granny glasses. "I can assure you Charles Joseph, we are not kidding. In fact, we've never been more serious."

Ms. Ferrell piled on. "It's your choice, Charlie Joe. Read ten books or write one. Whichever assignment you choose, it will have to be completed before the first day of school next fall."

It was a good thing I was sitting down, because otherwise I would have keeled over.

Read ten books or write one.

I was being asked to choose between the firing squad and the hangman.

But right away, I knew which one I was going to choose.

I was born a non-reader, and I was going to die a non-reader.

"I think I'll write the book," I managed to whisper mournfully.

A wave of grief, nausea, and disbelief washed over me. I'm pretty sure it's no exaggeration to say that my life flashed before my eyes.

Nice knowing you, world.

I had only one hope left. I turned to the two people who had raised me, fed me, sheltered me, protected me, and loved me. Now it was time for them to save me.

"On the up side, this means you can have your computer back," my dad said.

Part Seven
THIS IS THE LAST PART, I PROMISE

So now you know why I spent the whole summer writing a book.

* * *

I'm sorry the book didn't turn out the way I planned. I feel like I let you down.

It was supposed to be a Guide to Not Reading—but when you consider everything that happened, I'm probably the last guy that should be giving advice on that subject.

And it was supposed to be filled with really short chapters. But it turned out to have some not-so-short chapters after all.

I feel like in the beginning, everything was going great. I had, like, a zillion tips in the first few chapters.

But then the pages got longer. The chapters got longer. The sections got longer. Now that I think about it, it turned out to be exactly the kind of book I've spent my entire life avoiding.

Inexcusable.

Charlie Joe's Tip #24

NEVER READ A BOOK WITH A MORAL.

It's bad enough if you have to read a book. But books with morals are worse, because morals always involve behaving in an extremely honorable fashion, which we all know is completely unrealistic.

I don't need a book reminding me I'm not perfect.

I'm well aware of that already.

If this were one of those books that adults want you to read, there would be some sort of moral right about now.

But the only moral I can think of is, "never try to cut corners and have someone else do what you're supposed to do." (Especially if you end up getting caught and you receive a horrible punishment that ruins your whole summer.)

And if this were one of those books that you get assigned in school, it would have a happy ending, the kind where the kid says that writing this book was one of the most rewarding things he's ever done because it helped him see the error of his ways, and he's so thrilled to have discovered the joys not only of reading, but of writing.

But when it comes right down to it, this just isn't one of those books.

And I'm just not one of those kids.

* * *

But I will admit a few things.

I'll admit that writing this book—even though it totally wrecked my summer and quite possibly my life—wasn't the soul-killing, mind-numbing chore I thought it was going to be.

In fact, I've come to the conclusion that writing a book is far less annoying than reading one.

After all, I was allowed to pick my own topic, so I picked my favorite one: not reading.

And even though the book ended up being about a lot more than not reading, at least I was able to tell my side of the story, so maybe people like my parents and Ms. Ferrell would understand what happened, and not be so disappointed in me.

As my once-and-future best friend Katie Friedman would say, it was "therapeutic."

And even though I didn't exactly do what I set out to do with this book—and you have every right not to believe what I say—I can make you one last solemn promise.

When the new school year starts, I'm going to figure out a way to read as little as possible.

In fact, I already have a few ideas.

Don't tell anyone.

So now that I've finished the book,

I can finally relax for the rest of the summer.

Too bad school starts tomorrow.

✳ ✳ ✳

Did I mention that Hannah gave me my "Dead Babies" Beatles album cover back?

Yeah, that was pretty cool of her.

She dropped it off over the summer with a note that said "Thanks for everything. Love ya! Hannah."

The word *love* doesn't count when the word *ya* comes right after it.

✳ ✳ ✳

I haven't exactly been out and about very much this summer—I did have a book to write, after all—so I'm kind of looking forward to seeing everyone.

I hope they're looking forward to seeing me.

I'm looking forward to telling Jake he's more of a man

than I'll ever be, even when he's wearing his glasses, and how happy I am for him and Hannah. (Honest.)

I'm looking forward to seeing Eliza's new look, since she gives us something surprising every year.

I'm looking forward to that first-day ritual where everyone talks about the summer, and I'll say "I wrote a book," and I'll probably feel pretty proud when I say it, even though it was the hardest thing I ever had to do in my life.

And I'm even looking forward to seeing Mr. Obnoxious himself, Teddy Spivero, and telling him that this was the summer I finally fell out of love with his sister. He'll laugh in my face, and I'll insist it's true, and then I'll see Hannah and I'll probably fall in love with her all over again.

But that's okay. I'm still looking forward to all of that.

✳ ✳ ✳

Here's what I'm not looking forward to: getting my first homework assignment, and my reading list of books to read.

✳ ✳ ✳

But today—just today—it's still the summer. And my mom and dad said that since I finished the book, I could have my cell phone back, and I could do whatever I want.

The first thing I'm going to do is go outside and play with my dogs, Moose and Coco.

It's the least I can do.

Because during the worst times these last couple of months—when I was grounded for life, and I felt like the whole world was having fun except for me—the only thing that kept me going was seeing those two dogs looking up at me patiently.

"We have no idea what you're doing, you've never done anything like this before, but we still love you, and we'll wait as long as it takes," their eyes would say, taking pity on me as I sat at my computer. "We know that one day

you'll realize that it's summer, and that you should absolutely not be doing what you're doing. You should be outside playing with us."

They're absolutely right.

* * *

After playing with the dogs, I'm going to head down to the beach with my sister and lie there for a while, maybe go for a swim and have a soft-serve ice cream cone.

And then I'm going to text Katie and tell her to come meet me. And she'll text me back that she'll be there in fifteen minutes. And I'll text her back that I'm sorry that I wasn't around very much over the summer. And then she'll text me back and say I'm sorry for ratting you out, but you know what it's like in that crazy tiny chair sitting opposite big scary Mrs. Sleep. And then we'll text each other that we can't believe school starts tomorrow.

And then it will be tomorrow.

Charlie Joe's Tip #25

WHEN FINISHING A BOOK, NEVER LOOK AT IT AGAIN.

It's bad enough that you had to read this whole book. You don't want to be reminded of the experience.

Here are certain things you can do with a book once you've finished with it:

1) *Sell it at a tag sale.*
2) *If no one buys it, pay someone to take it.*
3) *Loan it to a friend. Forever.*
4) *Donate it to the school library.*
5) *Donate it to the town library.*
6) *Donate it to the Library of Congress.*
7) *Drop it in the bathtub.*
8) *Lose it. If someone finds it, lose it again.*
9) *Put it on the shelf behind the board games you never use.*
10) *Wrap bacon around it and give it to the dogs.*

Just don't intentionally burn it. That's off-limits.

But if it happens to slip out of your hands while you're reading by the fire? Well, then that's just the way it goes.

ACKNOWLEDGMENTS

I know, I know, more reading. Don't worry, I'll make it quick.

The following people made this book happen, and I'd like to thank them:

Michele Rubin and Nancy Mercado, Charlie Joe's godmothers, without whom he simply wouldn't exist.

The incredible team at Roaring Brook Press/Macmillan, friendly, funny, and fantastic.

JP, who nailed it.

Lauren Tarshis, who's been there, and who told me it was a good place to be.

Nancy Conescu, Maja Thomas, and Jeffrey Seller, who opened some doors along the way.

My colleagues at Spotco, the best place to work in the whole world.

Barbara and Jonny, for obvious reasons.

Kenny, Ellen, Jessica, and Jake, early adapters.

Ellen Kellerman, for being astonishing.

Claire and Chiara, whose students were both helpful and adorable.

Moose and Coco, for being the inspiration for Moose and Coco.

Charlie, Joe, and Jack, not huge fans of books, but huge fans of life.

Reluctant readers everywhere, for giving me inspiration.

And Cathy Utz, who is the beginning and end of everything.

GOFISH

TOMMY GREENWALD

© Suzanne Sheridan

What did you want to be when you grew up?
I don't remember, but it probably involved chocolate.

Were you a reader or a non-reader growing up?
I was a reader. My kids still haven't forgiven me.

When did you realize you wanted to be a writer?
Who said anything about wanting to be a writer? I wanted to be a television watcher.

What's your most embarrassing childhood memory?
Ages six through thirteen.

What's your favorite childhood memory?
Hitting every ice cream store in town with my grandmother. (Who's still alive, by the way—ninety-nine and counting.)

As a young person, who did you look up to most?
Everybody. I was a pretty short kid.

What was your favorite thing about school?
Making jokes in class that made kids laugh.

What was your least favorite thing about school?
Getting in trouble for making jokes in class that made kids laugh.

What were your hobbies as a kid? What are your hobbies now?
Then: Playing with dogs. Now: Owning dogs.

What was your first job, and what was your "worst" job?
I taught archery one year at summer camp. I'd never held a bow and arrow in my life. By the end of the summer, I still hadn't.

How did you celebrate publishing your first book?
By calling my wife and attempting to speak.

Where do you write your books?
The train, the library, Barnes & Noble. Anywhere but home. Home is for television and dogs.

What sparked your imagination for *Charlie Joe Jackson's Guide to Not Reading*?
My kids, Charlie, Joe, and Jack. They hated to read growing up. They hate it slightly less now.

Will we see more of Charlie Joe Jackson in the future?
I sure hope so. Do you? If so, please send cards and letters to The Charlie Joe Jackson Forever Project, c/o Macmillan Publishing Company.

What challenges do you face in the writing process, and how do you overcome them?
My desire to not work. When my guilt overcomes my laziness, I write.

Which of your characters is most like you?
Charlie's father.

What makes you laugh out loud?
The Daily Show.

What do you do on a rainy day?
Give thanks. An excuse not to exercise.

What's your idea of fun?
Watching my kids try their hardest at something.

What's your favorite song?
Depends on the week. This week? "I'm So Sick of You," by Cake.

Who is your favorite fictional character?
Fielding Mellish.

What was your favorite book when you were a kid? Do you have a favorite book now?
Then: *Are You My Mother?* by P. D. Eastman. Now: *Letting Go* by Philip Roth.

What's your favorite TV show or movie?
So many!! TV: *All in the Family, M*A*S*H, The Honeymooners, The Twilight Zone,* for starters. Movies: *Love and Death, Manhattan, The Shining.*

If you were stranded on a desert island, who would you want for company?
My family, as long as there was a desert school I could send the kids to.

If you could travel anywhere in the world, where would you go and what would you do?
Africa to go on safari. Some day.

If you could travel in time, where would you go and what would you do?
Eighteenth-century Vienna, to look over Mozart's shoulder when he was nineteen and writing incredible music.

What's the best advice you have ever received about writing?
My friend and agent Michele Rubin told me to change Charlie Joe's story from a picture book idea to a middle-grade novel.

What advice do you wish someone had given you when you were younger?
Stop eating Häagen-Daz when you turn forty.

Do you ever get writer's block?
Nope.

What do you want readers to remember about your books?
That books aren't the enemy.

What would you do if you ever stopped writing?
Feel guilty.

What do you like best about yourself?
My family.

What do you consider to be your greatest accomplishment?
Charlie, Joe, and Jack.

What do you wish you could do better?
Sleep.

What would your readers be most surprised to learn about you?
I'm the fifth funniest person in my family.

It's Report Card Day and Charlie Joe has another pretty lousy report card. Determined not to end up in summer school, Charlie Joe will stop at nothing to get those As!

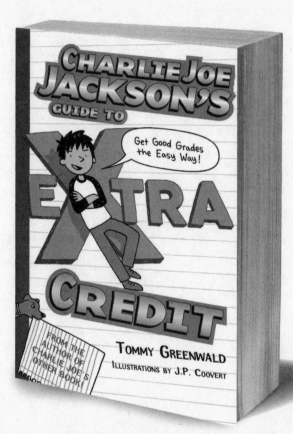

Find out what happens in
Charlie Joe Jackson's
Guide to Extra Credit
by Tommy Greenwald.

INTRODUCTION

How I ended up trying out for the school play is actually a pretty funny story.

Because if you know anything about me at all, you know I'm not exactly a "school play" kind of guy.

In fact, the idea of doing the school play is right up there with reading a book on my not-to-do list.

Which makes the fact that I was standing there on the stage of our middle school auditorium, singing a song about paper towels, all the more ridiculous.

And just because the most perfect creature in the world was trying out too—Hannah Spivero, of course—didn't make it any better.

"5-6-7-8!" yelled Mr. Twipple, the drama teacher. Even though most of us had no idea what those numbers meant or why he was shouting them at us, we knew it meant we should start singing the song.

So we sang:

Wiping up messes!
Brushing off dresses!
There's nothing paper towels can't do . . .

I looked at my friend Timmy McGibney, who was there, too. He looked at me. We were both thinking the same exact thing.

How did this happen?

I'll tell you how.

Two words.

Extra credit.

Charlie Joe's Tip #1

READ A LOT AND WORK HARD IN SCHOOL.

Reading and schoolwork are the backbone of every child's education.

It's extremely important to study hard and respect your teachers. The best way to make sure you get good grades is to do your work on time, and take great care and pride in everything you do. Try not to rely on extra credit if you don't have to, because it can turn out to be a very difficult process.

So, that's my first tip.

Or at least, it would be if we were living in fantasy land.

But we're living in real life, so ignore everything I just said.

Let's go back to the beginning: Report Card Day.

You probably already know that books and me don't get along.

And I'm not exactly what you'd call the most studious kid in the world.

In elementary school, that didn't really matter. I'd make my teachers laugh, and I'd participate in class, and I'd do just enough to get pretty good grades.

But everything changed in middle school. All of a sudden, the teachers expected me to actually read all the books and to pay close attention in class.

School turned out to be a lot more like school than it used to be.

Which is how Report Card Days became my least favorite days of the year.

"So what's the plan?" said my buddy, the ridiculously brilliant and unnecessarily hard-working Jake Katz. We were sitting at lunch. He asked me that every Report Card Day, as if I had some grand scheme to leave school in the middle of the day, go to my parents' computer, print out my report card (then delete the e-mail), find the nearest report-card-forgery expert and have him change all my C pluses to A minuses.

"I don't have a plan," I answered. Jake looked disappointed. I was pretty famous for my plans.

"My grades are definitely up this quarter," chimed in Timmy McGibney, my oldest and most annoying friend.

"That's super," I said, "but I don't want to talk about report cards right now."

I felt nervous, and I wasn't used to feeling nervous. I could usually get myself out of pretty much any bad situation, but going home to a lousy report card was kind of like going to a scary movie with your friends even though you hate scary movies. There was no way out.

I took a big swig of chocolate milk and immediately felt better. Chocolate milk is like that.

"Let's talk about something happy," I suggested, "like the fact that this is the last quarter of the year. Summer is right around the corner." Summer was my favorite time of year, by far. No school. No books. No report cards. There was absolutely nothing wrong with summer.

Then Hannah Spivero came up to our table and put her arm around Jake Katz, and I immediately felt worse again. Hannah Spivero is like that.

(Hannah, for those of you who have been living under a rock, happens to be the girl of my dreams. Only now, those dreams are nightmares, ever since she shocked the entire nation by deciding to like Jake Katz.)

Right behind Hannah was Eliza Collins and her adoring gang of followers, who I like to call the Elizettes. Eliza is the prettiest girl in school and has had a crush on me since third grade. The combination of those two things didn't make sense to anyone, especially me.

"Did I just hear someone mention summer?" Eliza asked. "What perfect timing! The girls and I have decided to form a Summer Planning Committee." Then she looked right at me. "It's coming up fast, and we need to make sure we have the best summer ever!"

Everyone cheered.

Eliza was used to people cheering in her presence, so she ignored it.

"The first meeting of the committee is this Saturday at my house, and you're all invited," she added.

Another cheer.

Hannah looked at Jake. "We have plans to go to the mall this Saturday."

I'll go to the mall with you, I thought.

"Maybe we can go to the mall on Sunday," Jake said. "The Summer Planning Committee sounds fun."

I couldn't believe my ears. Passing up alone time with Hannah Spivero went against everything I stood for as a person. "Okay, sure," Hannah said, but I could tell she was a little disappointed.

"What's wrong, Charlie Joe?" Eliza asked cheerfully. Since she liked me and I didn't like her back, seeing me unhappy always made her happy.

"Charlie Joe is feeling nervous about his report card,"

Timmy announced. He was another kid who enjoyed my misery.

"I am not."

Hannah put her hand on my shoulder, probably figuring she could help me forget my troubles and make me feel all warm inside from just the tiniest bit of physical contact. (She was right, but that's beside the point.)

"Oh, Charlie Joe, I'm not worried. You'll probably figure out a way to convince everyone that C's are the new A's. I'm sure your parents will be taking you to Disneyland by the time you get through with them."

Everyone laughed—it was a perfectly okay joke—but for some reason Timmy decided it was unbelievably hilarious, and instead of laughing he snorted apple juice through his nose and all over my fish sticks.

Great. Not only was I going to be nervous the rest of the day, I'd be starving, as well.

Timmy looked at the soggy fish sticks.

"Are you going to eat those?" he asked.

He'd eaten three of them before I could answer.